**W9-CTH-580**

*continued . . .*

## DEATH GETS A TIME-OUT

"Juliet and her patient husband make an appealing couple—funny, clever, and loving (but never mawkish). Waldman has an excellent ear for the snappy comeback, especially when delivered by a five-year-old."
—*Publishers Weekly*

"Waldman is at her witty best when dealing with children, carpooling, and first-trimester woes, but is no slouch at explaining the pitfalls of False Memory Syndrome either."
—*Kirkus Reviews*

"Think *Chinatown,* but with strollers and morning sickness. Arguably the best of Waldman's mysteries."
—*Long Island Press*

## A PLAYDATE WITH DEATH

"Smoothly paced and smartly told."
—*The New York Times Book Review*

"Sparkling . . . Witty and well-constructed . . . Those with a taste for lighter mystery fare are sure to relish the adventures of this contemporary, married, mother-of-two Nancy Drew."
—*Publishers Weekly*

"[A] deft portrayal of Los Angeles's upper crust and of the dilemma facing women who want it all."
—*Booklist*

## THE BIG NAP

"Waldman treats the Los Angeles scene with humor, offers a revealing glimpse of Hasidic life, and provides a surprise ending . . . An entertaining mystery with a satirical tone."
—*Booklist*

"Juliet Applebaum is smart, fearless, and completely candid about life as a full-time mom with a penchant for part-time detective work. Kinsey Millhone would approve."
—Sue Grafton, author of the Kinsey Millhone Mysteries

## NURSERY CRIMES

"[Juliet is] a lot like Elizabeth Peters's warm and humorous Amelia Peabody—a brassy, funny, quick-witted protagonist."
—*Houston Chronicle*

"A delightful debut filled with quirky, engaging characters, sharp wit, and vivid prose."
—Judith Kelman, author of *After the Fall*

"[Waldman] derives humorous mileage from Juliet's 'epicurean' cravings, wardrobe dilemmas, night-owl husband, and obvious delight in adventure."
—*Library Journal*

*Berkley Prime Crime Books by Ayelet Waldman*

NURSERY CRIMES
THE BIG NAP
A PLAYDATE WITH DEATH
DEATH GETS A TIME-OUT
MURDER PLAYS HOUSE
THE CRADLE ROBBERS

# THE
# CRADLE
# ROBBERS

_Ayelet Waldman_

BERKLEY PRIME CRIME, NEW YORK

**THE BERKLEY PUBLISHING GROUP**
**Published by the Penguin Group**
**Penguin Group (USA) Inc.**
**375 Hudson Street, New York, New York 10014, USA**
Penguin Group (Canada), 90 Eglinton Avenue East, Suite 700, Toronto, Ontario M4P 2Y3, Canada
(a division of Pearson Penguin Canada Inc.)
Penguin Books Ltd., 80 Strand, London WC2R 0RL, England
Penguin Group Ireland, 25 St. Stephen's Green, Dublin 2, Ireland (a division of Penguin Books Ltd.)
Penguin Group (Australia), 250 Camberwell Road, Camberwell, Victoria 3124, Australia
(a division of Pearson Australia Group Pty. Ltd.)
Penguin Books India Pvt. Ltd., 11 Community Centre, Panchsheel Park, New Delhi—110 017, India
Penguin Group (NZ), Cnr. Airborne and Rosedale Roads, Albany, Auckland 1310, New Zealand
(a division of Pearson New Zealand Ltd.)
Penguin Books (South Africa) (Pty.) Ltd., 24 Sturdee Avenue, Rosebank, Johannesburg 2196, South
Africa

Penguin Books Ltd., Registered Offices: 80 Strand, London WC2R 0RL, England

This is a work of fiction. Names, characters, places, and incidents either are the product of the author's imagination or are used fictitiously, and any resemblance to actual persons, living or dead, business establishments, events, or locales is entirely coincidental. The publisher does not have any control over and does not assume any responsibility for author or third-party websites or their content.

THE CRADLE ROBBERS

A Berkley Prime Crime Book / published by arrangement with the author

PRINTING HISTORY
Berkley Prime Crime hardcover edition / August 2005
Berkley Prime Crime mass-market edition / July 2006

ISBN: 0-425-20617-3

BERKLEY® PRIME CRIME
Berkley Prime Crime Books are published by The Berkley Publishing Group,
a division of Penguin Group (USA) Inc.,
375 Hudson Street, New York, New York 10014.
The name BERKLEY PRIME CRIME and the BERKLEY PRIME CRIME design are trademarks
belonging to Penguin Group (USA) Inc.

PRINTED IN THE UNITED STATES OF AMERICA

10  9  8  7  6  5  4  3  2  1

# One

NINE years ago, in preparation for my third date with Peter, I schlepped out to Queens on two subways and a bus in order to borrow a black lace bra from my friend Cindy Rappaport. And now? Now I couldn't even be bothered to scrape the baby spit-up off my T-shirt before crawling into bed. If my husband's hand had accidentally brushed against those parts of my body once seductively draped in expensive French lace, I would probably have chewed it off. I love Peter, I really do. It was only because I'm so crazy about him that I was at all concerned that our matrimonial bed had become as arid as the Oklahoma Dust Bowl. I understood the reasons for the drought, but I was far too drained and exhausted to miss the rain. At four months old, Sadie, our third child, weighed in at nineteen pounds. I realize that only other mothers of freakishly sized children have the infant growth charts burned into the insides of their eyelids, so let me provide a translation: Sadie was officially off the charts. So far off, in fact, that the nurses in our Los Angeles pediatrician's office recalibrated the scales every time we came for an appointment, positive there was some mistake. The baby had done nothing but nurse since she was born, and her need for constant access to my body meant that my husband was obliged to keep his hands to himself. His hands, and everything else.

"Don't even think of touching me," I said as Peter leaned in for a kiss. Then I pasted an insincere smile to my face. "I mean, gosh, honey, I'm just so tired tonight."

"So what else is news?" Peter said, sighing.

Before our current romantic crisis, I had assumed that I was the source, from both the nature and nurture sides, of my children's thespian talents. Those tremulous sighs, that bitten lip, the eyelashes wet with barely suppressed tears—hadn't I seen

2

those reflected back in the mirror all my life? Hadn't my own parents shown a truly remarkable fortitude in the face of precisely the same wiles? And yet here was Peter, giving my six-year-old daughter Ruby and her younger brother Isaac a run for their money in the drama queen department.

Peter sighed again, so loudly that it was almost a groan. I looked at him. He was sunk in the deep crevasse in the middle of our massive bed, staring at himself in the mirrored ceiling, and practicing his beleaguered husband expression. He'd become rather adept at it over the past few months. He looked downright wounded, so pathetic that I was almost willing to overcome my aversion to all things physical. Almost.

"The crack in the mirror is getting bigger," I said, to distract him.

"Are you serious? Where?" Peter's expression changed to one of concern, even panic. Ramon Navarro built our house in 1926. The actor lived in it for only a few years before he went on to more fabulous accommodations and ended up murdered in a Hollywood Hills mansion in 1968. The only reason we could afford the house was because it was not only completely run down, but a bit, well, quirky. The Latin lothario had had something of a baroque design inclination, and while touches like the basement dungeon, which Peter used as an office, and the Maxwell Parrish–style murals that seemed entirely innocent until you realized that the lovely young woman in the long pink gown sported a distinct Adam's apple and hands and feet that were a mite too big for a lady, were part of the charm of the house, we could have done without the mirrored bedroom ceiling. Our contractor had informed us, however, that as soon as we pried off the splintering glass we were going to have to deal with the ancient plaster crumbling above it, and the rotten floor joists above that. Until we had the desire and financial wherewithal to replace not just the ceiling but the floor of the third story above it, we were going to have to live with our reflected selves. Then the contractor made some joke about bordellos, which neither Peter nor I thought was funny, for obvious reasons.

Through necessity I had discovered that in order to distract Peter from thoughts of sex, I had to turn his attention to something potentially more disastrous, like the possibility that our slowly cracking mirrored ceiling was going to come crashing down on top of our heads.

Peter heaved himself onto his elbows and glared up at the crack. Our bed was also a legacy of the late Mr. Navarro, handed down to each subsequent owner of the house by virtue of the fact that there was no way to move the massive thing out. The room had clearly been constructed around it. Judging by its size, the entire house may well have been built around it. While I was quite in love with the intricately carved headboard, I would happily have bought a new mattress to replace the ancient and sagging one that was on the bed. It couldn't possibly have been the same one on which the movie star had entertained guests of various genders and professional and religious affiliations, but it sure smelled that way. However, nowadays nobody, it seems, makes a king and a half, and I hadn't yet gotten my act together to order a specially constructed mattress to fit the huge old bed. It looked like I was going to have to do it soon, however, because a series of tiny pink dots had lately appeared on Sadie's belly and back, leading to the inevitable conclusion that the mattress suffered from something far worse than mere malodorousness: an infestation of creepy-crawlies. Nothing like spending a king's ransom on a house only to find it populated by an entire nation's worth of invisible citizens.

"This house is going to kill us," Peter said. "It's going to crush us and bleed us like a succubus."

"I love our house."

"I love it, too, but it's still going to suck the life out of us."

"Hey, did I tell you that Isaac wants a King Arthur birthday party?" The second floor of the house had a series of Juliet balconies looking down into the living room. The flagstone floors and balconies made for the perfect setting for enacting the drama of the Knights of the Round Table.

"What a cool idea!" Peter said. "We can rent ponies and have jousting in the ballroom!"

Well, at least I'd succeeded in distracting him. The birthday party was well over month away, and my husband is something of space cadet, or a Luftmensch, as my grandmother would have said. His brain is in the clouds, his mind distracted by things like his next horror screenplay or his bid on an eBay auction for a Maskatron action figure (with three masks, a pair of weapon arms, and two flesh-tone thigh pieces). Within a month, neither he nor Isaac would remember this birthday party idea, and I would not have to tell them that if they thought that the cosseted preschoolers in Isaac's class were going to be allowed to hurl lances at one another, or that I was going to allow ponies in the house, they were out of their minds. Still, I was happy that at least Peter was finally thinking, however briefly, about something other than our sex life. Or lack thereof.

By morning, all three kids had migrated into our bed like refugees from a natural disaster. Except that the calamities they were running from were overpriced furniture, matching linens, and enough toys to populate a series of children's books. The only rooms in our house that were entirely furnished were the ones belonging to the three children. I'd spent an entertaining and expensive afternoon shopping from the comfort of my hospital bed while recovering from my last caesarean section. On the very day I realized we had actually found a house, I had purchased online everything I was missing for the kids' rooms, making sure it all matched. My mother, a woman whose photograph, with her trademark early 80s perm and brightly colored reading glasses, can be found in the *Oxford English Dictionary* under the word "frugal," never once bought matching bedroom furniture for me when I was a child. In fact, my bedroom "sets" were always inherited from the most recently deceased relative on either side of the family. I slept on Tante Froma's foam rubber mattress until I was nine, stored my clothes in Uncle Sol and Auntie Gertie's colonial chest of drawers until high school, and lived surrounded by my great-aunt Nettie's fascination for all things Danish Modern until I went to college. I swore that when I had children, my daughter would have a little white canopy bed with a matching dresser and desk. So far Ruby appeared not to care in the slightest about her lovely bedroom furniture and seemed only interested in wheedling herself into our bed whenever possible. Isaac could be sleeping in a shoebox for all he noticed his immediate surroundings. I had high hopes for Sadie, however, even though she had yet to spend more than the first two hours of any night in her carefully chosen Victorian-style crib with the pansy-print bumper and sheet set. She was bound to one day appreciate the fact that the knobs on her dresser matched the cushion on the desk chair, which were the same shade of sunny butter yellow as the linings in the baskets in which she would store her shoes, once she was big enough to wear them. Wasn't she?

I popped Sadie off the nipple and, holding my breath, shifted her into the bassinet pulled up alongside our bed. She belched softly, and then settled down. I exhaled, relieved at having for once made a successful breast-to-bassinet transfer, and turned to wake up the other two children. Then I heard a low rumbling. I turned back and the cloying sour smell of a breast-fed baby's dirty diaper accosted me. While I watched, a tangerine stain spread across the front of Sadie's pale blue onesie.

"I just don't get why it's orange," Ruby whispered. She sat up in bed next to me, staring into the bassinet.

"It's almost the exact color of your hair."

Ruby opened her mouth in a simulated retch. "Gross, Mom."

Sadie pursed her lips and sucked, still deeply asleep. This, I thought, is the biggest difference between a first-time mother and a third. Never, *never,* would I have allowed Ruby to lie festering in her own filth. Now, I wouldn't wake Sadie up if the house were burning down around us. I'd just wheel her outside in her bassinet and tell the firefighters to turn off their damn sirens.

"Go get dressed, kid," I said to Ruby. "If you're ready in five minutes or less, I'll make pancakes."

# Two

THE beauty of being a self-employed mother is that you can take your baby to work. That's also the horror of being a self-employed mother. Although, who am I kidding? I'm so barely employed that it hardly counts, and I certainly have no right to whine. (Not that that has ever stopped me before.)

I used to have a career. I used to be a criminal defense attorney working at the federal public defender's office in downtown Los Angeles. I represented drug offenders and bank robbers with the odd white-collar boiler room scam artist thrown in just to keep me on my toes. I loved my job. There was nothing I enjoyed more than a morning interviewing a client in the Metropolitan Detention Center, followed by an afternoon court appearance to argue a motion to reveal the identity of a confidential informant, topped off by an evening spent preparing a witness for cross-examination. It was when those days were complicated by pumping breast milk and racing home to see the baby before she fell asleep that the joys of work began to pale. I left the federal defender's office when Ruby was fourteen months old, full of plans to go with her to Mommy & Me, to sit with her on my lap at story hour in the library, to take long walks around the reservoir with her in the stroller, to laze away our days at the playground.

And that's what we did. Our lives were about Mommy & Me and the playground and story hour and crayons and building blocks. We went to the library, to the park, to the zoo, to the art museum. We made necklaces out of Cheerios and ate banana and almond butter sandwiches. Three days of that and I was ready to be institutionalized. In the years since then, I have gone on to prove that it is possible to be both so busy that you realize only at dinner time that you've eaten nothing all day but eleven frozen frappucinos and half a rice cake you found under the baby's car seat and, at the same time, to be so bored that a radio news segment on blind trout fishermen strikes you as the most provocative thing you've heard since college.

When I was pregnant with Isaac I began, accidentally at first, to do some investigation work. My husband says I was drawn to the work because I am nosy; he thinks that I have an unhealthy need to know what is going on in the lives of people around me. I think my natural curiosity is part of my charm. I'm nowhere near as bad as my grandmother, who stole Alice Roosevelt Longworth's famous line, "If you have nothing nice to say, come sit by me." I'm at least interested in finding out both the good *and* the bad about people. Is it my fault that the latter seems so much more prevalent and easier to discern?

Not quite two years ago, my old colleague Al Hockey convinced me to go into business with him. Al's not a lawyer. He's an ex-cop who retired from the force when the health consequences of the bullet he took made it difficult for him to function in uniform. He wasn't going to sit behind a desk and push a pen; that's just not the kind of guy he is. But the department wasn't about to let him back on the street with a crumpled colon and a chip on his shoulder. To be fair, the chip's been there all his life, and they shouldn't have hired him if they weren't interested in a cop who was constitutionally incapable of sucking up to the brass. After he quit the force, Al became a defense investigator with the federal defender's office, and then he went out on his own. Al and I are unlikely friends, but friends we are, and partners, too, although every so often I wonder if my excessive fertility isn't going to drive him to dissolve the partnership and throw me out on my ass. But I'm done having kids. Even if I wanted more, back then I wasn't letting Peter close enough to bring another Applebaum-Wyeth into the world.

"Any rats today?" I asked as I walked into Al's garage.

I'd tried to convince Al to shift our offices to one of the many bedrooms in my new house, but after glaring at the gargoyle chandeliers and homoerotic murals, Al had hopped back into his SUV and rolled on home to Westminster. I don't mean to imply that my partner is an intolerant man. Sure, he's a neoconservative nut, but his militia unit is the only racially integrated one in the United States. His wife is African American, and he is a card-carrying

Libertarian and thus adamantly in favor of things like gay marriage. As far as he's concerned, people can sleep with whomever and whatever they like, so long as the object of their desire is either a consenting adult or an inanimate object. He is, however, an old-school kind of guy, and certain things make him uncomfortable. Like the fact that my husband would be working underneath us in a dungeon with real handcuffs dangling from the walls and his storyboards propped up against an antique vaulting horse that none of us is naïve enough to think was ever really used for gymnastics. So it was the garage for Al and me, rats and all. Al insisted that the vermin infesting our makeshift office were *tree* rats, as if the fact that they normally made their homes in tall and gracious California palms made them any less disgusting.

"They've been quiet today," Julio, our office assistant, said.

"Please tell me you're not working on the computer."

"Of course not." He tapped a few keys and the screen went dark. One of the conditions of Julio Rodriguez's supervised release from federal prison was that he have absolutely no contact with computers. That's what happens when you've been convicted of immigration fraud through computer hacking. If being banned from the keyboard effectively means that you're barred from all employment other than the most menial, well, that's not the Probation Department's problem, is it? Al and I had been on a protracted and so far unsuccessful campaign to convince Julio's probation officer that society as a whole would be better served by harnessing this kid's significant technological talent than by forcing him to flip burgers or stand on a street corner waiting for day-laborer work. We were hoping that the fact that Julio never personally benefited from his hacking would count for something. The system he had manipulated belonged to the old Immigration and Naturalization Service, and he had been *giving away* Social Security cards, not selling them. But so far our pleas had fallen on deaf ears. The probation officer was of the opinion that whatever his motives, Julio was an incorrigible criminal with an addiction to Internet havoc and, like an alcoholic from booze, he needed to be kept away from the computer at all costs. While I thought the guy was overreacting, and I knew Julio wasn't about to commit another crime, I had to admit that there was a certain truth to the fact that our assistant could not, no matter how hard he tried, keep his fingers from dancing on the keyboard. In the couple of months since he'd started working for us, our network had already magically reconfigured itself and was now working at about four times the capacity and twice the speed. My hard drive had been restructured, too. I wasn't asking, but I knew it wasn't Al who had renamed and reorganized the database.

"Where's the boss?" I asked.

"Coffee."

"Ah." My partner is not much of a morning person and is as addicted to caffeine as Julio is to digital technology.

I sat down in my chair, pulled a baby blanket over my shoulder, and lifted Sadie out of her car seat. She wasn't crying yet, but she was making the snuffling noise that was a prelude to the frantic rooting for the breast that heralded the hysterical weeping. If I could cut her off at the pass, I might be able to get her to sleep for another hour. If so, it was possible that I would actually accomplish something this morning. That would be an event so unusual that it might cause my partner to fall to the floor in a dead faint.

"Anything new come in?" I asked.

"No," Julio said. "But Al is helping me with a personal problem."

My heart sank. It is so rare for a public defender to see clients turning their lives around. Julio, who had served his time and left prison with the fortitude and confidence to rewrite the story of his life, was the exception, not the rule. I couldn't bear the idea that his tale was going to be one with an unhappy ending.

"What happened?" I said.

"Don't sound so tragic," Al snarled from the doorway. His eyes were puffy from lack of sleep and he held a giant coffee mug in his hand. "It's not Chiki. It's his cousin." Chiki. Right. I reminded myself that Julio had recently, with an uncharacteristic blush and stammer, invited us to call him by his nickname.

"My cousin's bunkie."

"What's a bunkie?"

"That's what the ladies in prison call their cellmates. My cousin Fidelia is up at Dartmore. She called last night looking for help for her bunkie. The lady just had a baby, and someone stole the kid."

"Apparently," Al said, his old desk chair squeaking under his weight, "the girl signed the baby over to a foster family, thinking it was just supposed to be for a few days or weeks, and she's now afraid they've absconded with the child."

I shook my head. "Okay, hold on gentlemen. Back up here. Tell me what's going on slowly enough for my nursing-addled mind to comprehend it. Who are we talking about?"

"Her name is Sandra Lorgeree. She was just a couple months pregnant when she got busted, and she had the baby in prison," Chiki said. "She's doing five years."

"And her baby got put into foster care?"

"Not exactly," Chiki said. "California Department of Corrections regulations allow moms to spend just twenty-four to forty-eight hours with their newborns in the hospital after they give birth. Then the ladies get sent back to the prison. The babies got to be turned over to the custody of a blood relative. If the lady has no blood relative, then she has to find someone who is a foster parent licensed by the state of California. Otherwise the baby goes to the Department of Social Services and *they* put the baby in foster care."

"What's the difference who puts the baby in foster care?"

"This whole licensed foster parent thing has made things really complicated. It used to be that when a prisoner who had no blood relatives would have a baby, she could ask a friend to come up and get the baby and bring it back home. But now, the Department of Corrections won't release the babies to anyone who isn't a licensed foster care provider, even if that person is who the mom wants her baby to be with."

"But I still don't understand why this is 'baby stealing.' I mean, yes, it's awful and all that, but when the woman gets out she can just go get her kid, right?"

Chiki clucked his tongue in frustration. "It's real bad when DSS takes a baby, because as soon as they do, the clock starts ticking for termination of parental rights."

"What do you mean, 'termination'? Just because the woman's in prison? What if she's only serving like a year or something?"

Chiki gave me a look like I was the most ignorant person he'd ever seen. "If DSS get their hands on a baby, they only give the mom six months.

That's all. I know one lady, she got a three-month extension, but that's it. After that, the baby is gone."

I'm ashamed to say I didn't believe Chiki. I made a few murmurs of doubt, settled a sleeping Sadie in her car seat, and turned to my computer. With a few clicks of the mouse, I was reading a state statute that confirmed what Chiki had said. When a child up to age three is taken by the state, for whatever reason, the mother has, indeed, only six months to get it back. If she can't take the child back, she loses parental rights altogether. The idea behind this is a good one—infants should not languish in foster care, but instead should be adopted. But for women who are in prison, this requirement has devastating consequences. Once the children of a woman who is serving a sentence longer than six months enter the foster care system, she loses them forever, even if her sentence is only a year.

"This is awful," I said.

"No kidding," Al said.

"*You're* opposed to this?" I was surprised. Al was usually in favor of people sleeping in the beds they'd made, no matter how full of nails.

"You're damn right I am. The government has no right to take someone's child!"

"So what happened to Sandra?" I said.

Chiki said, "She didn't have no relative to take her baby, and no friend who was licensed."

Sandra had been at her wit's end, like many other women whose families lived too far away to make the trip to Dartmore prison, about sixty miles southeast of San Jose. All pregnant women in the state of California are automatically transferred to this isolated facility, as it's close to a maternity hospital. The fact that it's a maximum-security prison seems not to bother the California Department of Corrections overmuch. The social worker at Dartmore presented Sandra and other pregnant prisoners with what appeared to be their salvation. The Lambs of the Lord, a church-based foster care agency located in Pleasanton, a small city not too far from San Francisco, would send a family to take custody of their babies for as long as it took for the women to arrange alternative care. As soon as the prisoner's family or friends were available to pick up the baby, the agency would arrange transfer of custody. In the meantime, the baby would be safe, well cared for, and most importantly, out of the dangerous hands of the State.

Women immediately began signing on the dotted

line. At any given moment, somewhere between one and two hundred prisoners in California are in the advanced stages of pregnancy, and they're all shipping to Dartmore as they approach their due dates. Within weeks, the Lambs had dozens of grateful recruits, including Sandra Lorgeree. She turned her baby boy over to a sweet-faced young couple from the Lambs of the Lord a mere eight hours after he was born, and no one had seen the baby since.

"What does that mean, 'no one has seen him'?" I said. "Of course she hasn't seen him. She's in jail. Has someone else gone looking for him?"

"She's had people on the outside try calling the telephone number the foster parents gave her. They call at all different times of day and night, but no one ever picks up the phone."

"And that's why she thinks her baby's been stolen? Because the foster parents don't have an answering machine?"

Al said, "Jesus, Juliet." He heaved his feet onto his desk. "Since when do you have so much faith in the system? Usually you're the first person willing to believe that a prisoner is being victimized by the State."

I shook my head. "I just have a hard time believing that there is some elaborate baby-stealing conspiracy going on. I think it's much more likely that the foster family is a little overwhelmed with a brand-new baby and isn't answering their telephone. It doesn't seem that suspicious to me. How long has it been since Sandra had her baby?"

"Three weeks."

"Has she been in touch with the foster care agency? With the Lambs of the Lord people?"

"No, they don't accept collect calls. She's had friends call them from the outside, but they won't give any information out to anyone but the mother."

"How did she get in touch with them in the first place, if they won't accept collect calls from prison?" Prisoners can only call collect; they aren't allowed to use calling cards, and they have no access to cash. Frustratingly, the telephone companies that have the prison contracts charge a huge markup for those collect calls. Having an incarcerated individual call you can cost a small fortune. Still, most of the criminal defense attorneys I know begin their voicemail greetings with a message to the operator, informing her that "this machine accepts collect calls from prisoners." After I left the federal defender's office and my home number was the only one my old clients could use to reach me, our friends, family members, and Peter's business associates were greeted with the same salutation. It wasn't long before Peter got his own line.

Chiki, who had begun folding invoices into careful thirds and sliding them into pre-addressed envelopes, said, "She reached the Lambs of the Lord through the social worker at the prison."

"And has she talked to the social worker?"

"The social worker told her to stop making trouble or she'd end up in the SHU."

Nice. Threatening a grieving mother with the segregated housing unit. In which year of the master's program in therapy did they teach that?

Chiki gathered the envelopes together and put them in the out basket. Bright red, clearly marked in and out baskets were one of our organized assistant's many office innovations, and when Al wasn't filling them with the crumpled, greasy wrappings of In-N-Out burgers, they worked great to simplify the chaos in the garage.

Chiki said, "I told Fidelia you'd make a few calls, try to find out what happened to the baby."

"Oh Chiki, why did you tell her that?" I said.

Al said, "You got something else to do?"

"Man, you're grumpy today," I said as I glanced at my empty in basket. Our business was due to take a turn for the better any day, since we'd come under contract with Harvey Brodsky, flash lawyer to the stars. For a while Brodsky had circled around like a great white, sizing us up with a cold eye, stirring up the water with his churning tail, but not committing to the meal until he was absolutely sure we'd be a tasty enough morsel. Once we'd solved a high-profile murder and proved ourselves qualified to help get his clients out of trouble, he'd taken us on. So far all we'd done was a few routine checks on personal assistants and household staff, and one time Al had convinced his friends in the County Sheriff's Department not to charge a young client of Brodsky's for naked skateboarding at Papa Jack's skateboard park in Malibu. As Al had pointed out to the buddy of his who was on duty, the scrapes on the girl's behind were sufficient punishment on their own, and she *had* been conscientious enough to wear a helmet. Brodsky had been happy with that save. A front-page spread on the arrest would have ruined the young ingénue's credibility as this year's darling of the Christian rock circuit. The retainer money was coming in from Brodsky on the first of every month, but there was not, at this very moment, much of anything for me to do.

I pointed to Sadie. "I've got plenty to keep me busy."

"What's your problem, Juliet?" Al grumbled. "Poor woman's looking for her baby, and you won't help? This isn't the bleeding heart I know and love."

With Chiki around it was hard for me to admit to Al what was wrong. The truth was, I couldn't help but wonder if the baby wasn't better off, wherever he was. Don't get me wrong, I hate the idea of the state taking babies away from prisoners. It's terribly unjust, and the idea of a woman who is sentenced to a year in prison losing her baby because she can't reclaim it within this arbitrary six-month window is horrifying to me. But this friend of Chiki's cousin was going to be in jail for the next five years, and from what he was saying, she didn't have any real plans for who should take her kid. I didn't for one minute buy this paranoid baby-stealing fantasy of hers, but let's say, for a moment, that it was true. Let's say some childless couple fell in love with her baby and ran off with him. Sure, that's terrible, but some part of me that I was almost ashamed of couldn't help but wonder if the child wasn't better off, if he wouldn't be happier growing up in a family, ignorant of his birth mother serving out his early years in prison. The first five years of a child's life are important years, maybe even the most important. He needed a mother in his life, and he needed the security of knowing that that mother wasn't going to be taken away from him when his "real" mother was finally released from jail.

I was about to open my mouth when I looked at Chiki standing in the doorway, the Swiffer in his hands. Like most ex-prisoners, he liked to keep his surroundings not just neat and tidy, but almost compulsively clean. Perhaps he was like this before his experiences in prison, I don't know. It was an uphill battle in this garage, what with the rats and all, but the first thing Chiki did when he started to work for us was transform a storage unit in a corner of the garage into a utility closet, complete with spray bottles of every form of cleaner available at the market. He was partial to aromatherapy. His favorite implement was definitely the Swiffer, and he swished that thing around three or four times a day, catching up every bit of dust before it had a chance to settle on the floor. Chiki was a very young man when he went to prison, just out of his teens, slightly built and delicate. I never asked him what happened to him on the inside. I did not need to.

Now, as I watched him indulge his grim OCD, I thought of the young mother in prison, and the promise Chiki had made to his cousin and to her. I looked down at my own baby, safe in her nest of blankets in the car seat, her lips pursed in her sleep.

"I'll make some calls," I said.

"Thank you, Juliet. Fidelia will really appreciate it, and so will Sandra. I really appreciate it. You know, it's so hard for those ladies inside."

"Yeah, I know, Chiki. It's hard."

# Three

THAT night was book club, and even though I was nowhere near done with the book, I decided to go. I was feeling guilty about not having managed to reach anyone at the Lambs of the Lord, despite leaving a dozen progressively more irritated voicemail messages. I needed the company of some girlfriends, and if previous experience was anything to go by, I wasn't going to be the only book club member derelict in my belletristic duties. In fact, there were a few who had never once, in the six months we'd been meeting, managed to get through a novel, even when we'd chosen *The Da Vinci Code* expressly to guarantee them a simplified and propulsive literary experience. This month's novel was *Rabbit at Rest,* by John Updike, selected by the wife of a client of my best friend Stacey, solely for the purposes, I'm convinced, of announcing to the group that her husband's screen adaptation had just been greenlit. Which she had done eight times so far, by my count. And we hadn't yet met to discuss the book.

Stacey and I were at Greenblatt's, a delicatessen on Sunset Boulevard in West Hollywood, not too far from my house. In addition to decent pastrami, Greenblatt's has what Stacey insists is the best selection of fine wine in the city. If I were on my own I would have stopped at the Safeway and picked up something in "red" or "white," but my oldest friend has a far more epicurean palate. Stacey has always been a classier girl than I; even at college she had already developed a style that, together with her shimmering good looks, intimidated every single person on campus, male or female. We became friends despite the fact that Stacey had riding boots especially constructed for her feet and I was a Jersey girl who thought the sale rack at Abraham & Strauss was the height of luxury. It helped back then to cement our friendship that I was as smart as she was. We competed on an even keel for a while, until I dropped onto the mommy track and she stayed on the bullet train to superstardom, becoming one of the most successful agents at International Creative Artists. What keeps Stacey and me together is loyalty and love. For all our differences, I know I can trust her with anything, even the grimmest and most repulsive secret of my life. She would stand by me through it all. And I feel the same way about her. Still, I can't help but be jealous of the fact that we seem to be on opposite trajectories. Like a normal person, I get fatter and more wrinkled as we creep inexorably up the ladder of our thirties. Stacey gets thinner and ever more dewy and luminous. Pretty soon people are going to start thinking I'm her mother. And then, inevitably, her grandmother.

"This is what I'm bringing," she said, holding up a bottle of Château Guiraud Sauternes 1990.

"Oh come on, Stacey. That's a fifty-dollar bottle of wine."

"No, it's a seventy-dollar bottle of wine that I'm getting for fifty bucks. If you tell the ladies that it was on sale, I'll kill you."

Catering our book club has become something of a competitive sport. I lay the blame squarely on

Stacey. The first night she was hosting, she had to work late to close a deal, and instead of whipping up a pot of pasta or picking up some cheese and crackers at the supermarket, she instructed her assistant to arrange dinner for twelve. It was the young woman's first and last week on the job, and I can still taste the poached lobster in ginger sauce. And that was just the first course. Since then, each hosting member has felt the need to ratchet up the level of hysteria, and the books we read are fast becoming beside the point. Pretty soon we'll be dipping truffle fingers into foie gras. We've already done the blinis and caviar.

The guests were each responsible for a bottle of wine to complement the hostess's largesse, which explained our little shopping excursion. I picked up a bottle from the sale bin. "I'm bringing this. Long Vineyards Johannesburg Riesling. Eighteen dollars. Perfect. Generous, even. Maybe I can find something for under ten."

"Just buy the wine, Juliet," Stacey said, tottering off in the direction of the cash register. I gazed longingly at her shoes. I think one of the things I miss most about working full-time as an attorney is the freedom to spend ridiculous sums of money on shoes. It's hard to rationalize the expenditure when your days are spent on the playground or in a garage in Westminster. I fantasized for a moment about doing a worker's compensation stakeout in a pair of Marc Jacobs slingbacks. I inevitably end up peeing in the bushes at least once or twice during a long day trapped in my car outside a malingering employee's house, and I somehow doubt the designer took squatting and spraying into account when creating his satin prints. He definitely didn't construct them for climbing up to the top of a play structure to retrieve a stranded toddler. And they aren't finger paint–repellent. I've actually proved that. Or rather, Isaac has.

Book club was in full swing by the time we arrived. Mine was by far the cheapest wine offering and, to Stacey's dismay, hers was not the most expensive. Someone had left the $140 price tag on a bottle of Perrier-Jouët. I was quite relieved that I'd scraped off all evidence of my parsimony. Still, I don't think my mother has *ever* spent even eighteen bucks on a bottle of wine. In my family, if it's over $7.99 and has a cork, we keep it for a special occasion.

Our hostess for the evening was someone I'd introduced to the book club. I'd met Frances at this little swim school I'd been taking the kids to for the past few years, way over in West L.A. The lessons are fifteen minutes long, which wouldn't give you enough time to get to know someone unless you were a woman with small children used to cramming an intimate conversation into the time it takes to change a diaper. While her little boy and my two kids were paddling around in their flippers and wings and bobbing after rubber dinosaurs to the cheers of their pathologically good-natured college student instructors, Frances and I sat side by side in the shade and exchanged life histories. By the time Ruby was jumping off the diving board, I knew everything about Frances, from the complications of her mother's third divorce to the frustrations her husband felt at having been passed over for partner at his law firm. Best of all, I'd gotten lots of free medical advice. There's nothing that pleases a hypochondriac so well as an obliging new physician friend. Frances hadn't practiced since her daughter was born, but she was a gynecological surgeon by training and we'd already discussed everything from prolapsed uteruses to incontinence to fibroid tumors. Not that I suffered from any of those ailments, but you can never be too prepared.

Tonight, however, Frances was showing off her skills as a sushi chef. She'd prepared a lavish spread of raw and cooked fish and Japanese salads and rice, and was handing out bamboo mats and sheets of seaweed. The other women all valiantly attempted a variety of maki rolls, but I kept to the hand rolls and was soon contently balancing a heaping plate on my lap.

Playing with our food loosened us up even more than usual, and by the time the heated sake and various wines were passed around, the gossip had already started. Inevitably, as is always the case when a group of married women in their thirties gathers, conversation began with our children and moved quickly to our husbands. There was one woman in the group whose spouse was female, but somehow that didn't seem to matter; she complained right along with the rest of us. Rachel bitched about how her husband would walk in the door every evening after being at work all day and announce that he needed time to "decompress" in front of the television before being forced to deal with her or the kids. "Honestly," she said, "sometimes I just feel like pitching the baby at his head and taking off. When do *I* get to decompress?" Nods all around at that one.

Colleen was on a tear about her husband's new passion—his rock and roll band. "They practice every weekend. Every single weekend. He's a thirty-seven-year-old orthodontist, and suddenly he thinks he's Eric Clapton. And when I dare to suggest that maybe he should consider missing practice so that he could go to Nicky's hockey game, then I'm the old lady who's bringing him down. He gives me this adolescent grief, like I'm his mother!"

"I wish Zach would miss Dylan's games," Beth said. "He gets absolutely insane about soccer. You guys had to sign that positive cheering pledge, didn't you?" We had all signed the league's pledge to cheer on our children using only affirming and encouraging words. "Well, I *laminated* ours and put it on the fridge. It hasn't done any good. Zach still stands there on the sidelines screaming like a maniac. And poor Dylan just keeps running back and forth pretending he can't hear anything his father is saying to him."

I opened my mouth to tell the women about my own aging adolescent, with his thousands of dollars' worth of superhero toys and his comic books. The truth is, however, that I find that part of Peter's personality endearing. I knew from our very first date that he was an overgrown child—he'd shown up with a Fantastic Four button clipped to his lapel. But he'd also had a bouquet of irises in his hand. Peter is almost always willing to share his toys with my other children. And, frankly, he is a whole lot better at playing with Ruby and Isaac than I am. No, the difficulties we were experiencing had nothing to do with his immaturity.

"I just have to ask this question," Katherine, our resident lesbian, said suddenly. "How often do you guys, you know . . . do it?"

The women all laughed, and a few groaned. We'd all had this conversation before. Whenever women gather to talk, the topic inevitably bubbles to the surface. The deep, dark, not-so-secret secret of contemporary American marriage is that nobody is having any sex.

"We've had sex three times," Kristina said.

"This *week*?" I asked, stunned. I didn't know anybody who was having sex three times a week. Those were pre-kid numbers.

"No. Three times. That I can remember. Donovan, Bianca, and Trenton. Three kids, three times. That's it." She didn't look like she was kidding.

"Has anybody actually tried making a date for sex like all the magazines suggest?" Lucy asked. Lucy is another mom I met on the circuit. Our daughters are in the same class, and she has a son a year younger than Isaac. Lucy is one of those beautiful Los Angeles women who manage within weeks of giving birth to be back in their hip-hugger jeans and midriff-baring tops. I hate her.

"Yeah, right," Frances said. "Date night. Give me a break. That's invariably the night the cat decides to vomit in our bed or one of the kids has a four-hour temper tantrum. Or the baby-sitter's husband gets arrested and she needs to go to Riverside to bail him out. Date night never happens. And anyway, the problem isn't *making time* for sex. The problem is *wanting* sex."

Katherine said, "I don't have a sex drive. But neither does Amy, so we don't really have a problem. That's one of the many nice things about being a lesbian. Bed death is a mutually agreed-upon phenomenon."

Rachel said, "Well, that's certainly not true in my house. Ben never stops complaining about it. Never.

It's become a running gag with him. If I hear one more joke about hookers, I'm going to kill him."

"Do you know," Kristina said, "the other night we were out with two couples for dinner and one of the men actually made some crack about how the guys ought to all get together and split the cost of a prostitute. They talked about it for ages. Where they'd get her, who would go first. I finally had to tell them to shut up. They were pretending to be kidding around, but I'm not the only one who sensed more than a dash of seriousness in the conversation."

"The danger is always there," Stacey said, her eyes fixed to the maki roll she held delicately between vermilion-polished nails. Stacey and her husband were back together again, but they have been separated more than once. Andy strays, usually with a younger and less accomplished version of his wife. It's not hard to figure out that he finds Stacey intimidating, that her beauty and success emasculate him to some degree. Men like Andy are made uncomfortable, even frightened, by a woman's intelligence. I read a study once that showed that for men there is a 35 percent increase in the likelihood of marriage for each 16-point rise in their IQ. For women, there is a 40 percent drop for each 16-point increase. Obviously Andy isn't alone in desiring a bimbo.

Stacey's warning cast a momentary pall over the group. Jeannie, who is a few years younger than the rest of us, spoke up. "Our sex life is still pretty terrific," she said.

"You don't have children," Kristina reminded her.

A pretty rose stain spread across the young woman's cheeks. "We will soon," she said. "I'm pregnant."

"Well then kiss your libido good-bye."

That's what we were giving her in lieu of congratulations? "Oh, Kristina," I said. "It's not necessarily true. I was voracious when I was pregnant. After I got over all the throwing up. And before the reflux and the hemorrhoids really kicked in. I wanted it all the time!"

Katherine said, "When was that, exactly? When you had no nausea, reflux, hemorrhoids . . ."

Lucy added, "Or varicose veins, restless leg syndrome, swollen ankles, migraine headaches . . ."

"Or yeast infections, unusual body odor, cramping, vaginal dryness . . ." Beth laughed.

"Don't forget the full-body itching!" Colleen

said. She was days away from giving birth. "I've been itching for months, even with enough prednisone to turn this baby into an East German weight lifter."

"Stop it!" I said. "The poor woman is, what, three months pregnant?"

"Eight weeks," Jeannie whispered.

"Eight weeks!" I said. "Don't terrify her. She's all aglow. Maybe she won't suffer from any of our symptoms. And anyway, we were talking about sex. *Sex*. Not full-body itching or yeast infections."

"Oh, she's never going to have sex again," Colleen said. "She might as well get used to *that* now."

"Doesn't anyone want to talk about the book?" Barbie whined. "I prepared a whole series of questions for the group based on my analysis of the characters. As you know, my husband is adapting the book for the screen and has already been signed to direct it himself. Let's start with the end."

"Wait!" I said. "I haven't finished it. Don't give anything away."

But she didn't hear me. "Wasn't Rabbit's death, like, the most poetic thing you've ever read?"

# Four

LAST month, after I rear-ended someone on the 10, Peter made me promise not to use my cell phone while driving. The nice young man I bashed in to was also talking on his cell phone, so he couldn't condemn me as easily as my husband did, but it's true, I'm a bad enough driver without the additional distraction. Still, much of an investigator's work is done on the phone, even in the computer age, and I spend an awful lot of time in my car. Luckily, there was a long wait on the pickup line in front of Ruby's school. I handed Isaac a juice box and half a peanut butter sandwich, popped Sadie onto a breast to catch a little mid-flight refueling before we set off for tae kwon do, and called the office. I had asked Chiki to put the word out to his family that if Fidelia called, they should find out if she knew of any women who were now out of custody who had had experiences with the Lambs of the Lord. I wanted to do everything possible to avoid a plane ride up to Pleasanton to the foster care agency's office, and since they weren't answering my calls, I thought an old client might be the best way to find out about them.

"I've got a name for you," Chiki said. "Fidelia doesn't know for sure, but one of the other women behind her in line for the phone said she heard about this lady whose baby was taken by the Lambs of the Lord. The lady got out and is living in Canoga Park, in the Penfield Avenue projects."

"What's her name?"

"They called her Sister Pauline. No one could remember her last name, but her mother's the head of the tenants' commission out at Penfield Avenue. They knew that for sure. They said Sister Pauline used to brag about her mama all the time."

"Okay, I'll find her. Canoga Park. It figures." In the middle of the night on Christmas Eve, it would take me half an hour to get all the way out to

Canoga Park. After school on a weekday? There was no way I could make it there and back during the kids' tae kwon do class, even if I signed them up for an extra half hour of sparring.

"Chiki," I said. "Do me a favor: Fax requests for legal interviews with Fidelia and Sandra Lorgeree up to Dartmore for me, just in case I have to go."

Ruby bounced into the car, tossed her backpack in the front passenger seat, and whacked her brother on the side of the head. He screamed, the baby woke up from her nursing stupor, and it took me a good ten minutes to get everybody calmed down and buckled into their car seats and boosters. I'm sure Ruby announced her presence in the car so violently because she was trying to make known her opposition to her booster seat. While I had many failings as a mother, God knows, I was not willing to add to them crippling my child in an automobile accident. I had already sworn she was going to sit in a booster seat until she was tall enough and heavy enough to be safe without one, or until she got a driver's license, whichever came first.

I realize that forcing Ruby and Isaac to change into their tae kwon do uniforms while we were in transit somewhat diminished the security of the ride, but they kept their seat belts on, and we were running late.

I dropped Isaac in Mighty Mites and took Ruby up the stairs to the yellow and green belt class. She had just moved up to green, after struggling for quite some time with a mere green stripe on her yellow belt, and she was full of herself, swaggering onto the mat and giving the American and Korean flags a crisp bow. I scanned the assembled crowd, seeking out a mother I knew well enough to ask for a favor, but one whom I hadn't imposed upon yet. There was one: a dark-haired woman with a shelf of a bosom and a roll of stretch-marked belly peeking out from between her tight T-shirt and her army-green, paint-spattered capri pants. She wore dark eye shadow and mascara and a slash of purple lipstick. Her hands were smudged with what looked like charcoal. She looked like an artist, or a Hollywood rendition of one. I recognized her from Isaac's preschool—her son was a year ahead of mine.

"Hi, Karen," I said.

"Karyan," she said.

So much for the favor.

She said, "Remind me of your name? I know we've met at preschool, but when I'm working on a piece I get so distracted. I have a hard time remembering things."

All was not lost. "Oh, that's totally fine. Really. I'm terrible with names myself. Juliet. Juliet Applebaum. And my son is Isaac. He's a year below . . ."

"Jirair."

"Jirair, of course. So, do you guys live around here?"

Three minutes later, I was pulling the booster seats out of my car, dumping them into Karyan's, and setting off for Canoga Park, having set up a tae kwon do car pool, commencing that afternoon. The only trick would be ensuring that Peter was home to greet the kids when Karyan dropped them off, because I was going to be stuck on the freeway heading out to pay a call on a woman named Sister.

Finding Sister Pauline was easier than finding a parking space outside the projects where she lived. It wasn't that there wasn't any place to leave my car. The problem was that someone had managed to break a bottle against nearly every available curb, and I didn't relish the thought of changing a tire as the sun set over Canoga Park. Finally, I pulled the car into the parking lot of a 7-Eleven and offered the clerk two dollars to let me leave it there for longer than the allotted thirty minutes. We settled on five bucks, but I made him promise to keep an eye on the car. It wasn't like I *really* thought anyone was going to take a joy ride in my minivan, but I'd only had it since Sadie was born, and despite the dent I'd already put in the bumper, I didn't want it stolen. More because I didn't want to have to cab it home from Canoga Park than because I had any special fondness for my car. It already smelled too weird for that.

The kids playing double Dutch on the cracked asphalt driveway alongside the housing project not only knew where the tenants' commission president lived, they knew her daughter Sister Pauline, and they knew that she was home.

"She always home," one little girl said, bobbing her head. Her hair was woven into a mass of braids, swirled into a pattern over her skull. I love braids, but whenever I attempt them on Ruby's red curls I end up making her look like a circus clown.

The little girl pointed me in the direction of a ground-level apartment. "You Sister Pauline's parole officer?" she asked. "I never seen a parole officer with a baby before."

I had clicked Sadie's car seat into the Snap N Go
stroller—perhaps, in my opinion, the most important invention since the disposable diaper—and
draped my diaper bag over the handlebars. The little
girl was right—I did not look much like a parole officer, or an investigator, for that matter. I prefer it
that way. Nine times out of ten, rather than impede
my work, having a baby or child along ends up being helpful. Children act as a nice little smoke
screen when I want to interrogate a witness—people
are rarely defensive when questioned by a woman
with a couple of kids hanging off her. Other women,
in particular, are put at ease by it. A cute toddler has
gained me access to homes whose thresholds, had I
been on my own, I wouldn't have been allowed even
to cross, never mind been given a glass of milk and
a plate of homemade oatmeal raisin cookies once
inside. I'm careful not to put my kids in harm's way,
however, and if once or twice I've had to pierce a
juice box and hand it into the backseat while tearing
down Venice Boulevard in pursuit of a suspect, well,
I do my best to exceed the speed limit by only what
is reasonable under the circumstances. I'm very
careful. Okay, so when I was pregnant with Isaac I
did get shot, but I've learned a lot since then.

The woman who answered the door was honey-skinned with a dusting of freckles across her nose and cheeks. She wore her hair ironed into waves. She looked to be in her mid-twenties and was carrying a young child on her hip. The little girl was about three or so, with eyes so round and wide she could have been a model for a Keene drawing, that is if the Keenes had ever painted African American children.

"Can I help you?" she asked.

"Sister Pauline?"

She narrowed her eyes slightly. "Can I help you?" she repeated.

"My name is Juliet Applebaum, and I'm a private investigator representing a woman who is incarcerated in Dartmore. My client's newborn baby is in foster care with the Lambs of the Lord, and she has some concerns about the organization. She thought you might have had experience with them."

"Who's your client?" She held the door with her hand, not even allowing me to see into the apartment.

I tried to size her up. I didn't want to reveal Sandra Lorgeree's identity if there was any chance of trouble. In prison, the web of debts owed and grudges held is very complicated. I needed to tread carefully. "I don't think I'd better say, Ms. . . . I'm sorry, I don't know your last name."

"Hubblebank."

"Ms. Hubblebank. I have to preserve my client's privacy."

"What about my privacy? Why you think I should tell you anything if you won't even tell me who you working for? How I know you not just working for the Lambs of the Lord, trying to set me up?"

I paused and chewed thoughtfully on my lip. "You're right. It's not fair to expect you to give me information with nothing in exchange. How about this. You let me bring my baby in out of the sun, and we'll sit down and talk. I'll tell you all about what happened to my client, and if you feel comfortable, you can share your story with me."

Pauline looked at Sadie and her face softened. "How old is she?"

"Four months."

"She big."

"Don't I know it."

"This one big, too. She only twenty-two months old."

"She's not even two yet? I was sure she was three!"

Pauline shook her head, smiling. "No. Not even close. She big because I nursed her. All my friends thought I was crazy, but my mama put all us kids to her breast, and I knew I wanted that for my babies. Breast milk's the best thing for them. You giving your baby breast milk?"

I motioned toward my inflated chest. "Can't you tell? This is *not* my normal look, I promise you. I nursed all three of my kids—my boy until he could *talk*. He was so hard to wean I was afraid I'd end up pumping bottles until he was in high school."

"I never did that. That pumping thing. They gave me one of them at WIC, but I'd squeeze and squeeze and nothing would come out."

"Oh, those hand pumps are terrible. I rent a monster electric one. It's bright yellow and I feel like a Guernsey dairy cow hitched up to a milking machine, but it's the only way. You could use a hand pump for a week and not get enough for even one feeding."

Pauline shook her head. "I just took her with me wherever I went. Until I went away. You can come in. You'll want a glass of water before you nurse that baby."

Pauline, her mother, and Pauline's young daugh-

ter shared a one-bedroom apartment that was designed around a shrine of photographs of a man in a
police officer's uniform. The pale blue velvet sofa
and matching recliners all faced the altar; the television on its cart was angled toward it. Even the small
dining table in the dining area had an empty place at
its head, leaving a clear line of sight from every
chair to the grouping of photographs, the framed officer's badge, the parchment police academy graduation certificate, and the wall of award citations.

I left the stroller wheels in the tiny front hall and
brought the car seat and sleeping baby into the living room with me. I sat down on the edge of the
sofa and put Sadie on the floor at my feet. The wall-
to-wall carpet was thick piled shag, worn in places
and covered in odd spots by woven throw rugs. I
supposed that the rugs covered stains or tears.

Pauline handed me a glass of ice water and
placed a platter of corn chips and a small bowl of
salsa on the table. "We don't have any mild," she
said, sitting down on a recliner and settling her
daughter in her lap. "And I don't think the spicy's
too good for your milk. Maybe you should just have
the chips plain."

"Thanks," I said. "Plain chips are great."

"My other baby, she a little older than yours."

"Your other baby?"

"Not this one; not Dericia. Taniel, my younger baby. The one you asked about. The one the Lambs of the Lord took. Next week, on the eleventh, that's her seven-month birthday." Pauline rested her chin on Dericia's head. The little girl wiggled off her mother's thighs and ran to the television set.

"Dora?" Dericia said, patting the TV screen. "Time for Dora?"

"Okay, baby," Pauline said. "But go watch in the bedroom." Dericia ran out of the room and her mother turned to me. "I don't like for her to see me cry, and I can't think about Taniel without crying."

"She's bright," I said.

"Just like her sister. I know my Taniel is smart like Dericia."

"You were pregnant with Taniel when you went inside?"

She nodded. "Only just. I didn't know for sure until after I got arrested. And then I thought for sure I'd be out before I had her. I didn't expect no fifteen-month sentence, I'll tell you that."

I knew enough not to ask what she had been convicted of. That's a rule with prisoners and ex-prisoners. If they want you to know their offense, they'll tell you. Otherwise, you mind your own business. But Pauline was willing to share.

"I took fifteen months on a crack-cocaine charge. Pled to it, finally. My lawyer, he said if I went to trial I'd get lots more. Still, it seems like a long time away for just half a gram of crack, don't it?"

"Yes, it does."

"My mama, she nearly died, she was so ashamed. My daddy, he was a police officer. That's him over there. He died when I was a girl. Just had a heart attack one day in bed. He wasn't but thirty-six years old. Sometimes I think it's better he died before he had to see me go to jail."

I didn't know what to say.

Pauline sighed and her eyes filled with tears. "Prison wasn't even the worst part of it. Losing the baby. Losing my Taniel. That's a life sentence."

I shifted forward in my seat, leaning toward her. "What happened, Pauline?"

She wiped her eyes. "Call me Sister Pauline. That's what people call me. My mama was all set to come up and get Taniel, but the problem was, you see, she don't drive. She was going to have to wait for my uncle Daniel, the one I named the baby for, to take off work. Up in prison they only give you a day in the hospital and there just wasn't going to be any way for Uncle Daniel and my mama to get up to Dartmore in time. The social worker"—Sister Pauline's lip curled—"that evil woman, she arranged for the Lambs of the Lord man to come visit me. He told me they'd send a foster mother for my baby and she'd keep her until my own mama got up to Dartmore. I was so happy I found them." She laughed bitterly. "I was so afraid that if DSS got hold of my baby they'd never let her go. I never thought that the Lambs would take her. Never for a minute."

By now she was weeping freely, tears streaming down her face. She rubbed the back of her hands on her cheeks. I wanted to get up and hug her, but there was no room for me on the recliner next to her, and there was something self-contained about this young woman in her grief.

"What happened when your mother came up to get Taniel?"

"She never got up to Dartmore. My uncle Daniel, he fell off a roof the week before Taniel was born, and he broke his back, so he couldn't drive her nowhere. The family that took Taniel, they kept telling my mama when she called, 'Oh take your time, she doing fine.' Mama looked for someone else to drive her on up. Then *she* got sick. She lost her foot to the diabetes. Her friends on the tenants' commission took up a collection to send her up to Dartmore, but it took almost six months before she was well enough to go get my baby. Right before she went up, I got this letter saying that there was a hearing scheduled to terminate my parental rights. My mama got herself to the hearing. She told the judge I was going be getting out in just three more months, but by then it was too late. The judge just gave my Taniel to that couple, the Lambs of the Lord people, saying that I'd abandoned her and that she'd be better off with them, that that woman was her mama now."

Sister Pauline's story chilled me. Was that possible? Could a baby be signed over just like that?

"Tell you something else," Sister Pauline said. "I know why they wanted her; I know why they wanted my Taniel."

"Why?"

"The social worker brought those people to the hospital room to pick up Taniel at the end of my day with her. I found out after that they weren't supposed to be there, but they were there, right in my room. I had my baby girl to my breast, just to give her some little bit of milk before she had to go, and the woman, she gets this pinched look on her face when she sees that. The social worker tells the nurse to show them my baby, and then the nurse takes Taniel away from me and hands her to the foster mother. Taniel's all wrapped up in a little striped blanket with her little pink hat on her head and the lady says to her husband, 'Oh look! She so fair! She looks just like a little white baby.' Those people stole my Taniel because she came out with my light skin. If only her daddy been dark, like Dericia's daddy, I'd still have my little Taniel. I know I would."

At that moment Dericia ran into the room, squealing a line from her TV show, "Swiper no swiping!" at the top of her lungs.

Sister Pauline leaned down to scoop her daughter into her lap and I stared at the pair. Taken separately, her story and Sandra's could have, if not a benign explanation, then at least an understandable one. In Taniel's case, if you closed your eyes to the chilling racism of the foster mother, you might argue that the family had simply fallen in love with their foster child, and after six months no longer wanted to turn her over. In Sandra's case, if there even were a case, and not just a series of missed phone calls, the argument could be made that the foster parents were worried about the well-being of a child who would be taken from them after five years. Each case independently had its merits. However, when taken together, suddenly there seemed to be a terrible and troubling pattern. Were the Lambs of the Lord conspiring to take the babies of incarcerated women at Dartmore Prison?

# Five

AL had his tie flipped over his shoulder and was holding not one but two chili dogs, one half eaten, grease soaking into the bun and dyeing it fluorescent orange.

"I don't understand how you can eat that at nine in the morning," I said.

"How is this different from huevos rancheros? Or bacon and eggs?"

"It just is."

He shook his head balefully. Normally, I can follow Al on any of his culinary expeditions. Together we've eaten at canteens and dives from Santa Barbara down to La Jolla. But I cannot eat a Pink's chili dog, no matter how crisp the skin on the thin sausage, no matter how fragrant the hot sauerkraut, no matter how crunchy the chopped onion, first thing in the morning. Even if I know that that is the only time of day you can count on the chili in the steam table not to settle into a pool of thick, orange grease. In three hours, or even two, I would have been right there with him, and I might even have been convinced to give the jalapeño dog a try. But all I want at 9 A.M. is a cup of coffee and a donut. Two donuts, maybe.

Al unhinged his lower jaw and stuffed the remains of his first dog into it. Then he started in on the second. "So are you more inclined to believe Fidelia's bunkie given what you learned from that Pauline woman?"

I shrugged. "Filing for termination of parental rights isn't exactly baby stealing, although it's pretty damn close. And the way they went about it is worth investigating, that's for sure. But not by us. This is something the Department of Social Services should be looking into. Or the U.S. Attorney's office, if the agency is engaged in some kind of civil rights violation. I'm going to make some calls, see if I can't motivate one of those agencies to take over the case. I'll get in touch with some people at the U.S. Attorney's office and call the Department of Corrections. I'll file a report with DSS, too. And while I'm at it, I'm going to prepare a request for information from DSS and from family court for any information they have on Sandra's baby's foster care placement. The might have some record of the specific placement, even though it was contracted out through the Lambs of the Lord."

Al smacked his lips and licked the last bit of mustard from his fingers. "I'm still hungry. Maybe I should get some fries."

"God no," I said. "This place has the worst fries in the city. Come back to my house, I'll feed you something."

Al and I were at Pink's because I didn't want to head all the way down to Westminster, a good thirty miles south of the city, if all I was going to do was spend my day making phone calls. I had tried to lure him north with more reasonable breakfast foods, but it had taken a chili dog to get him out of his house.

Although I'm not a cook—Peter is responsible for that in our family—I keep my cupboards stocked for Al's infrequent visits, and soon enough we were set up on either end of my long dining room table, between us an array of carbohydrate- and salt-laden snack foods. We were each busy on the phone, trying to convince someone in a position of authority to pay the slightest bit of attention to the fact that there was something strange going on with the Lambs of the Lord foster care agency and the women prisoners of Dartmore Prison.

My attempts to rouse the interest of someone in the United States Attorney's office in Los Angeles met with exactly no success. That shouldn't have been a surprise to me. I did not have many friends in that office. Lots of people I knew from Harvard Law School went on to become Assistant United States Attorneys, far more than joined the public defender's office, but once we found ourselves on opposite sides of the courtroom, our friendships cooled. There is, in federal court especially, a certain cordiality, a civility that is expected between defense attorneys and prosecutors, but anything more than that is difficult to maintain. First of all, clients never like it when their public defenders are too chummy with the government. They have a hard enough time believing that a lawyer they don't pay is going to do a decent job for them. If I had a nickel for every time I was told that the next time around my client was going to get a "real" lawyer, I could probably buy myself a car. A small one. Maybe a Hyundai. But a car, nonetheless. Secondly, after enough cases where the system seems stacked against your client, and the U.S. Attorney seems not only to relish the inequality, but to take advantage of it, it's hard not to develop some animosity of your own, especially in drug cases. There was an assistant U.S. Attorney with whom I'd gone to college who seemed unperturbed by the irony of aggressively prosecuting drug offenders whose conduct was not much different from things she did herself when we were both undergraduates. It didn't even seem to bother her that I had been a witness to her debauched youth, but as I'd made my disgust at her hypocrisy abundantly clear, and had even, in a fit of anger over a particularly bitter plea negotiation, threatened to report her to the bar association for, and I quote, "Being a drugged-out, lying bitch, with a coke habit to rival the Columbian cartel's," she wasn't inclined to take my calls.

"I have burned too many bridges," I said to Al, as I hung up the phone for the fifth or sixth time.

"That's not true," he said. "It's only the shysters

who hate you. The U.S. Marshals think you're cute. And even the FBI agents like you."

"Not the ones I've cross-examined."

"That's true. The one's you've had on the stand call you a ball-breaker."

"They do not!"

"This is news to you, girlie?"

I shrugged. "No."

It wasn't, really. I could hardly pretend to be ignorant of my own aggressive courtroom style, although I had always tried to cloak it in a veneer of sweetness. I'm small; barely five feet tall, and I found out early on that if I came on too strong it came off strangely, like I was some kind of angry leprechaun. I always dressed the part the jury expected me of me—simple suits, Peter Pan collars, velvet headbands. I smiled at them, recruited Peter to sit proudly in the first row behind the bar. I patted my clients' hands, smoothed their shirts, even hugged them, hoping that the members of the jury would say to themselves, "If that sweet little lawyer likes the six-foot-four-inch biker with the skull and crossbones tattooed on his bald head so much, how bad can he possibly be?" It was a surprisingly effective strategy. I got mean only on cross, and then I really did go in for the kill, tangling the witnesses up in their own lies. That was easiest to do with the confidential informants, liars one and all, but it was shocking how often the law enforcement officers felt comfortable twisting and stretching the truth. They hated when I tripped them up; it made them look bad, it made the judge angry, and often it cost them their convictions. And agents, be they FBI, DEA, ATF, or any others, live and die by their arrest and conviction records.

"You get anywhere with the CDC?" I asked. State prisons are all managed by the California Department of Corrections, an all-powerful organization that determines everything from how a prisoner's time will be calculated to where she will serve her sentence.

Al shrugged. "I got shuffled around. Office of Health Services. Different management sections. The chaplains' service, for goddamn's sake. Nobody's interested. I even asked if I could file a request for a formal investigation. They have no such procedure."

I called the Lambs of the Lord number again. I knew it was a futile effort, but I left another voice-mail message. Then I looked down along the table to where Al sat drumming his fingers on the scarred wooden surface. "I've got to go up there, don't I?" I said.

"Yup."

"This is going to cost us."

"Yup."

"Why are we doing this?"

Al shrugged.

"Where's the money going to come from?"

Al sighed. "We'll pull it out of expenses. It's important to Chiki."

"Why is it so important to Chiki?"

"Because it's important to Fidelia, and she's family."

I think this is why, of all the clients we represented at the federal defender's office, Al chose Julio Rodriguez—Chiki—to take under his wing. They share this deep and abiding certainty that a man does whatever he has to, at whatever cost, for his family. It wasn't just the Robin Hood–like nature of Chiki's crime that Al so admired. It was the parents, siblings, cousins, aunts, and uncles who showed up to every single court appearance, filling the courtroom, silently lending their strength to the young man who stood quaking in an orange jumpsuit and shackles. Al, whose own parents and sisters had never spoken to him after he married an African American woman, whose daughters did not know their cousins, was overwhelmed by this large, loving, and multi-hued Mexican American family.

"You coming up to Dartmore with me?" I asked.

"Nope."

"Why not?"

"Someone's got to be here in case we get some actual paying work."

I sighed.

He dug in his jacket pocket and pulled out a pack of orange Stim-U-Dents. He stuck one in his teeth and smiled.

"Going up where?" Peter stood in the arched doorway leading down to his dungeon, blinking his eyes like a mole feeling sunlight on his face for the first time.

Just then, Sadie, who had been sleeping since we got home from Pink's, began screaming. I'd left her in her car seat in the front hall and I ran to get her, relieved at having a moment longer to figure out how to explain to my husband that he was going to have to juggle all three kids on his own while I set off on a wild goose chase, on a case where there wasn't even going to be a paycheck for Al and me.

When Sadie and I returned to the dining room, we found Al packing up his bag. My husband and my partner tend to have that effect on each other. They drive one another out of rooms. It's not dislike, exactly; it's more like they have absolutely nothing in common and neither can really figure out what I see in the other guy.

"Al, do me a favor," I said. "Call Chiki from the car and tell him to buy me a ticket for the early shuttle. If I can catch the nine A.M., I can be up and back in a single day."

After Al left, I found Peter standing in front of the refrigerator, sizing up its contents with his mouth twisted into a comical frown.

"What do you want for dinner? Pickles or soy sauce?"

"I forgot to go grocery shopping," I said. "Let's just order pizza. Can you watch the kids tomorrow? For the day?"

Peter shrugged, closing the refrigerator door. "That's pretty much a rhetorical question, isn't it?"

I sighed and shifted the baby in my arms. "I'm

sorry honey. I know I shouldn't have just sprung this on you, but it looks like something pretty awful may be going on up at Dartmore, and I need to go up there and get some more information."

He poured himself a glass of water from the sink. "Al told me about Chiki's cousin's friend and the baby. It sounds awful, but why didn't *you* tell me about it, Juliet? I mean, you've been working on this thing for days, and this is the first I've heard about it."

Was this true? Had I really not told Peter about the case? We hadn't talked about much of note in the past couple of months; our conversations were limited to who was taking what shift with the children.

Peter took a long drink and then put his glass down. With his eyes on the glass, rather than on me, he said, "It's just, you know, I'm really lonely, Juliet. I can't remember the last time we made love."

Of course, how silly of me. Here I was, worrying about how little we'd been communicating, when this was the *real* problem. What was really bothering my husband wasn't that he didn't know about my caseload. What was bothering him was what was bothering all the husbands. If only he were getting it regularly, he'd be contently whistling his way through life, satisfied with himself and with his marriage. He was lonely not because we were drifting away from one another, talking less, acting as foremen responsible for swing shifts in a baby factory. No, that didn't bother him at all. What bothered him was that he wasn't getting any action.

"If I'm going to be gone tomorrow, I'd better pump some more milk," I said, handing him the baby. "I'm not sure I have enough in the freezer for a whole day away."

# six

At seven the next morning, I was pouring coffee down Peter's throat, trying to jolt him into consciousness so that I could walk out the door with Chiki, who had not only bought my ticket but shown up to drive me to airport. He was sitting awkwardly at my kitchen table, trying to keep from staring at the gargoyle wall sconces that were hung at odd intervals along the wall over the dark cabinets. We couldn't find the right size light bulbs, and had just stuffed normal bulbs into the mouths of gargoyles, so they all looking like they were choking on large, round, glowing objects.

"One more cup, honey," I said, pressing a mug

into my husband's hand and scratching his scalp. His eyes drifted closed and I pinched him. He jerked awake. Peter works at night, writing down in his dungeon until two in the morning, sometimes even later if he's on a deadline. He never gets up before ten, and would much prefer not even to see the sun before it begins its afternoon descent in the sky. Sometimes I wonder if he writes horror movies because he himself is a creature of the night, most comfortable in the dark. Ever since he'd started working in a dungeon, I'd been a little worried that he was going to turn into an actual vampire.

"I'm going to die," he muttered.

"You are not. Okay, listen. There are two bottles of fresh breast milk in the fridge, and one on the counter. The bottle of milk on the counter is from this morning. I just pumped it, so it can stay out for a few hours. Like, six to eight even. But you'll end up using it before then. After it's done, use the bottles in the fridge. Once you've given her a bottle, you should put it back in the fridge. Don't leave it out, because bacteria from her mouth can grow in the milk. But don't throw it away. I don't care what the books say. I'm not throwing out a whole bottle of breast milk just because she took two sips. Change the nipple before you give it to her again. That's good enough. After you're done with the bottles in the fridge, move on to the bottles in the freezer, but only take those out one at a time, because they spoil faster and I don't want to defrost them unless absolutely necessary. You got all that?"

"Which milk do I use first?"

"Oh for God's sake, Peter! Listen," I recited the instructions again, and watched the haze of confusion descend more firmly on his face. I sighed. "How about if I write it all down. How about that?"

"Good idea," he said, slurping his coffee.

While I was digging around in the kitchen drawer for a pen that had not had been chewed past the point of utility, the doorbell rang.

"Who could that be at seven in the morning?" I said, going to the front door.

I pulled open the massive oak door with the bronze knob the size of one of my children's heads. The man standing on my front steps towered over me. He was close to two feet taller than I am, and three times as broad. My kids could have used his large white sneakers for kayaks and his belly jutted so far out in front of him that he had to extend his ham hock of an arm way out past it to reach the gong that served us as a doorbell.

"Stanley?" I said. "Stanley, what the hell are you doing here?"

"Morning, Juliet."

"Stanley, please tell me this is a social call. Please tell me that you're dropping by to thank me for the Dodgers tickets Al gave you last season. Please do *not* tell me you are standing on my front steps because you are about to serve me with a subpoena."

"No, Juliet. I'm not serving you."

"Thank God. Because that is *all* I need."

"I'm serving your husband. Is Peter home?"

I glared at him. Then I called over my shoulder, "Hey, Peter, remember I told you about that process server Al and I refer business to sometimes? That old *friend* of Al's from when he was on the force?"

Peter grumbled something unintelligible.

"Well, you'd better come out here because he's got a little present for you."

*"What?"* Peter came flying through the front hall, his ratty old fleece bathrobe flying out behind him like a Batman cape. He grabbed the papers from Stanley.

"You'll forgive me if I don't come in, Juliet,"

Stanley said. "I'd prefer if my first visit to your home were under different circumstances."

"I am *so* not asking you in, Stanley."

"I didn't remember until I saw you standing there that your husband's name was Peter Wyeth. Otherwise I would have called. I sure would have. You know I would have."

I sighed. "You want a cup of coffee?"

"No, thank you. Excuse me, Mr. Peter Wyeth?"

"What? What?" Peter said.

"You've been served, sir."

"He knows he's been served, Stanley."

"I am aware that he knows that, Juliet. But you know I've got to verify service for the record."

I shook my head. "You're going to be picking up the lunch tab next time, Stanley."

"I am certainly aware of that, yes I am."

"See you later, Stanley."

"Good-bye now. Have a good day, Mr. Wyeth."

I watched Stanley heave his massive body down the path to the canary-yellow Cadillac DeVille he has been driving for as long as Al has known him, and probably for a lot longer than that. When I turned back to my husband he was holding the wad of stapled documents out to me with a trembling hand.

"I'm being sued!"

"I know."

"What do you mean you know? How did you know?"

"Calm down, honey. It's not like Stanley works for Federal Express. He's a process server. Ergo, you're being sued. Who's suing you?"

"A maniac! A maniac I've never met. I can't make heads or tails of this. Read it. Read it right now and tell me what the hell is going on."

Having a criminal defense lawyer for a spouse gives a person the opportunity to see the justice system in all its baroque and bureaucratic glory. Before he met me, Peter did not understand how long a case can drag out, how much is involved in a trial, how much can be at stake. Civil litigation is hardly the same as criminal: still, watching me prepare obscurely worded motions dealing with barely comprehensible concepts like habeas corpus, forfeiture, motions for preliminary injunction, and the like, convinced Peter that the American legal system is far more like the absurdly haphazard Court of Chancery of Charles Dickens's *Bleak House* than it is like the home of reason and logic that we all learned about in grade school.

I took the complaint out of his hands and scanned it quickly. "Okay, first of all, it's not just you who's being sued. It's you and your production company and the studio. So that's nice. You've got some company. Not to mention indemnification."

"But what is this crackpot claiming?"

I flipped the pages, walking back to the kitchen with Peter trailing behind me. "Hmm."

" 'Hmm'?" he shouted.

"You're going to wake the baby." After nursing pretty much nonstop from five to six in the morning, Sadie was asleep, not that I cared. I was leaving. If Peter woke her, it was his own problem. "The crux of the claim seems to be that he pitched an idea for an animated cannibal TV series to the studio about ten years ago, and he says you ripped off his pitch."

"But my animated series is based on my movies!" Peter's series of cannibal horror movies have been pretty successful, as far as B horror movies go; they have a devoted cult following. A live-action TV series once made it all the way to a pilot, but it was never picked up. Now there was an animated version in the works, and for the past few months Peter had been consumed with critical decisions like whether to go with CGI or traditional animation.

"Yes, well, he seems to be saying that you stole your movies from his pitch to the studio."

"But that's insane. My first movie came out years ago. And it was a script that I shopped around all over town. And it wasn't even made by this studio. They just bought the distribution rights!"

"The plaintiff claims that all that was an elaborate ruse. He claims that the studio got so excited by his pitch that it secretly contracted with you to write a screenplay, which you then pretended to make with a small independent production company but really made with the studio's money just so that you could make the sequels large enough so that you could go forward with the animated TV series. Which was the plaintiff's idea. Which you stole."

Peter collapsed into his kitchen chair. "This is insane. It's is going to go away, right? Please tell me this is going to go away."

"It's going to go away. It's going to cost the studio some money to litigate, and I hope to God they don't decide to settle, but yes, it's going to go away."

"Settle? Settle? But it's all a lie! How could they settle?"

"In order to avoid spending a quarter of a million dollars in legal fees. But let's not go there, okay? I mean, your studio is famous for not settling, otherwise it would end up a constant target for these kinds of extortionists, and it's a patently false claim. Don't worry, honey. The lawyers are going to take care of it. It's going to be all right."

Peter groaned.

"Sweetie," I said. "Chiki and I have to get going or I'm going to miss my flight. Are you going to be okay here?"

He groaned again.

"Peter," I said. "Let's focus now, okay? Sadie? Ruby? Isaac?" I kept the words very simple. "Can you handle this? Do you want me to stay?" I made my unwillingness to do that so clear by the sound of my voice that the hopeful expression on his face immediately faded.

"No, I'll be fine," he said.

"Call Lilly if you're in trouble," I said. "She's in town this week, and I'm sure she'll let you come over this afternoon and hang out by the pool." Our friend Lilly Green is a movie star with a full staff of nannies. When left on his own, Peter often resorts to Lilly's beneficent companionship. But then, so do I. It's a lot easier to kill a day with three children at *her* house than at ours. Especially since at her house you get to lie on a chaise longue drinking iced tea while a nanny takes care of your children.

"You are going to help me with this lawsuit, aren't you, Juliet?" Peter said.

"Of course I am. And there's not going to be anything to do. Tomorrow I'll call the studio's legal department, but I'm sure they're already dealing with it. They'll make it go away. I promise."

He stood up and gave me a hug. I kissed him lightly on the cheek. "Honey, Chiki and I really have to go. See you tonight."

"I'll be waiting."

# seven

THE visiting room of Dartmore Prison made an attempt at cheer that somehow served only to highlight how grim the place really was. The long tables had been pushed back from the walls in one corner to allow some floor space to be transformed into a play corner where a few children played listlessly with broken plastic toys. The Duplo buckets contained too few building blocks to make a satisfying castle, and the ride-on fire engine was missing a wheel, so the toddler using it had to cling to the seat at a perilous angle, pushing with his chubby sneakered feet and squeaking along half-heartedly across the dingy tiled floor.

The attorney visiting rooms were located along one wall of the main room. They were even more bleak than the main visiting room—claustrophobically small, with glass doors so that the guards could be sure that no untoward activity was taking place inside.

I called down both Fidelia and Sandra, and while I waited for the guards to find them, frisk them, and bring them in, I thumbed through a *Vogue* magazine I had bought in the airport. Every prisoner was subject to a thorough body cavity search both before and after a visit, and depending on where she worked in the prison, and how long it took to locate her, it could take as much as an hour for a visit to begin. I had time to read all about how it took Kate Hudson *weeks* to get back into her size 28 jeans after having her baby, and how she still needed to lose twenty more pounds. Since I couldn't fit one of my *breasts* into a pair of size 28 jeans, let alone my behind, I wasn't feeling all that sorry for Ms. Kate. Still, her fat little naked baby caused me to get one of those dangerous nursing mother reactions, and I had a terrible feeling I was going to have to run outside and use the breast pump I had left in the rental car in the parking lot. I'd pumped once in the bathroom on the airplane, a decidedly unpleasant experience (what *is* that smell in airplane bathrooms?), and once in the parking lot before I'd come in the prison. That had been fairly comfortable, the cigarette-lighter adapter easy to use, and I would have been fine if a small boy hadn't popped his head in the passenger-side window I had rolled down for air, causing me to shriek and spill breast milk all over my pants. He had been nearly as frightened as I, and his grandmother even more horrified. The stain on my slacks made me look like I'd wet myself, and I had a feeling that if the air-conditioning in the visiting room didn't start working soon I was going to begin to smell pretty funky. Just the way to inspire confidence in a client. Well, I reminded myself, it wasn't like I was being paid for my work on this case. They'd have to take me as I was. Stinky, the eighth dwarf. Although if it took them much longer to get down here I was going to have to be rechristened Leaky.

Fidelia was the first to arrive. She was a tiny woman, even shorter than I am, with rabbity features and a broken front tooth. She passed her tongue over that tooth over and over again as she talked, as if irresistibly drawn to the sharp edges of the angled crack.

"Chiki, he tell you what I'm in for?"

"No, of course not."

Fidelia was happy to talk about it. She had been a senior in high school, two months past her eighteenth birthday, when a boy, someone with whom she'd "hooked up" on a fairly regular basis, decided that he didn't like the fact that she was hooking up with other guys. Or maybe he just didn't like her smile that day. Whatever it was, he came after Fidelia with his fists, broke her nose, and gave her two black eyes. Fidelia showed the purple of her bruises to her brother, and her brother showed the silver of his automatic pistol to the boy. Fidelia's brother got twenty-five to life for murder. Her sentence was lighter; she could get out in as little as fifteen years.

"Fifteen years," I said. "That's a long time."

"Yeah. But I got my friends. Sandra, she's a good woman. She's smart, too. She helps all of us with our cases. She's better than a lawyer, you know? There's another lady inside who's a real lawyer, like went to law school and everything, and Sandra does a better job on our appeals than Clarisse does. And

Sandra don't charge nothing. Clarisse, you got to pay her, or get someone on the outside to pay her. Sandra, she don't even ask the girls for cigarettes or shampoo or nothing."

"Have you two been roommates for a long time?"

"Since before Noah was born. That's her baby. Noah Anthony. We from the same neighborhood in L.A., Eagle Rock, but of course we never knew each other on the outside. Sandra, she had a white bunkie before me, but that lady she got all hooked up with the Aryan Women, and Sandra, she hates them. She fought that girl until they put her in the SHU and then they sent her over to me. That was messed up; Sandra, she could have been killed. The Aryan Women, they're part of the Aryan Brotherhood, and those guys run the prison, you know? But Sandra, she didn't care. She said they could kill her, but she wasn't going to spend the next five years living with no Nazi lady."

When I was done talking to Fidelia, and had sent her back up, they let me see Sandra. In normal company, she would not have seemed so gargantuan, but in the land of the Lilliputians, compared to Fidelia and me, she loomed like a basketball center. Despite the pits of acne scars on her cheeks, Sandra was beautiful, blonde, and regal, with a long nose and aquamarine eyes, like some kind of Nordic princess. She held her feet splayed, her back straight, and her small bosom thrust out, in that stately posture of a woman whose childhood included years of ballet lessons. She was carrying the usual pile of legal papers and envelopes.

After we introduced ourselves, I asked her about what Fidelia had said.

"I never said anything about not wanting to be bunkies with that woman."

"You *did* want to spend five years living with a Nazi?" I said.

"Of course not. I just didn't take any such stand. I was nowhere near that brave. I simply asked to be transferred, repeating my request until the warden got so irritated with me that she had me put in the SHU for two weeks. By the time I was released, my former roommate was in segregation, having stabbed someone in the throat with a knife made out of toilet paper." Sandra sat down.

"Toilet paper?" I said.

"Sure."

"I've heard of making knives out of tooth-brushes, hard candies, spoons. Never toilet paper."

"It's like papier-mâché," Sandra said. "Ms. Applebaum, I understand from Fidelia that you have agreed to investigate the disappearance of my baby. I am very grateful to you. You cannot imagine how horrible it is to be stuck in here with no way to find him, no way even to know if he is safe."

"Chiki told me about how it happened that Noah was . . . was taken. But could you tell me yourself? Just so I'm sure I have the full story?"

She folded her hands on the table in her front of her. She had a stillness about her that was remarkable, especially considering the fact that I could tell she had been a junkie, and a hardcore one at that. I did not know if she was currently using, but I could see that Sandra had used for long enough to blow out the veins on the inside of her elbows and even those on her wrists. There were marks on her forearms, on the side of her neck, in the well of her throat. Her pale skin was a roadmap of heroin ruin.

"In the months before Noah was born I tried to find someone to take him. My parents both passed away—my mother when I was young, in grade school, my father almost five years ago now. My father has no family, but I have an aunt and two cousins on my mother's side. I haven't seen them since I was a teenager, but I know if I had some time, I could find them."

"What's your aunt's name?" I asked.

"Bettina Trudeau. And my cousins are Jonathan and Mary. I don't know if Mary got married and changed her name.

"It's an unusual enough name, Bettina Trudeau. I should be able to find it with a simple skip trace."

Sandra smiled sadly. "I hope you'll need to." Then she continued with her story. "I heard about the Lambs of the Lord from the social worker here at the prison. Some of the other pregnant women in the unit were using them, and it seemed like the perfect solution for me. The Lambs could keep the baby for as long as it took for me to find my aunt or my cousins. They sent me a packet and I signed a foster care agreement with them."

I frowned. "Did the social worker arrange for them to send you materials?"

Sandra nodded. "A week or so after she told me about the Lambs of the Lord, I got their stuff."

"So you didn't contact them? The social worker set it up for you?"

"Yes."

That, it seemed to me, was going to be important in any lawsuit against the organization and against that social worker. If she was actively soliciting on behalf of the Lambs of the Lord, and going so far as to set up contracts with women who had not actually contacted the Lambs of the Lord themselves, that would directly implicate her in the baby-stealing conspiracy. If one existed.

"What's the social worker's name?"

"Brock. Taylor Brock."

I jotted that down.

"Does she work here full-time, do you know?"

"Mornings, I think, most days."

"Did you bring the paperwork you got from them?"

Sandra took an elegant brochure printed on thick, creamy paper from one of her creased envelopes. She had brought dozens of these envelopes down with her. Prisoners aren't allowed to have file folders, so they keep all their papers in the envelopes in which they receive them. I've known prisoners to carefully nurture a single manila envelope for a dozen years. For that reason, I always make sure to send each page of correspondence in its own large envelope. Just in case they need an extra one.

Sandra had a contract on matching paper, replete with fine print. There was also a form entitled "Instructions for Transfer of Custody." I glanced over the documents, noticing the engraved letterhead and the organization's address.

"Did you ever meet with anyone from the Lambs of the Lord?"

"Just the foster family. When I got to the hospital I called the number on the instruction sheet. The foster parents got there right away, but the midwife wouldn't let them take my baby. She said I had a right to at least a few hours with Noah."

"A social worker wasn't there to facilitate the transfer?"

"No, just the couple."

I shook my head and motioned for her to continue.

"It was a long labor, and I was so tired. I tried not to, but I fell asleep holding Noah in my arms. I wasted hours of his time with me, sleeping. But I remember it. I have reconstructed every single moment of those hours in my mind. Those are the only minutes in the first years of my son's childhood that I will be with him outside of a prison and I want to remember them exactly as they happened."

I swallowed, willing myself not to cry, and swearing that I would linger with gratitude and joy over my baby as soon as I once again held her in my arms.

"After about six hours the couple came in," Sandra said.

"What were they like?"

"Young. Nervous. I don't know. It was hard to pay attention. Everything happened so fast. I was staring at Noah, trying to hold him in my eyes for as long as possible. They sort of whisked him out and away. I didn't even talk to them, really."

"And what's happened since?"

"I've written to the address they gave me, but my letters have come back 'addressee unknown.' The Lambs of the Lord won't accept collect calls, but I've written to them, too. They wrote me this letter."

She opened an envelope that had softened and crumpled a bit over time, but was scrupulously clean and unmarked. She pulled out a single sheet of paper. The letter, on plain white paper with what looked like a totally different letterhead, laser-printed rather than engraved as it had been on the formal contract and the solicitation, informed Sandra that the Lambs of the Lord had no record of her case, that the child "Noah Anthony Lodge" was not under the care of the agency, and that all further correspondence from her would be returned unopened.

"I wrote back to tell them they had the name wrong, that it's Lorgeree, not Lodge. I've asked friends on the outside to call the telephone number the foster family gave me, but nobody has gotten through. The same with the number for the Lambs of the Lord. Noah has just vanished. Sometimes I wonder if I've gone crazy, if this was all some horrible psychotic episode. If it wasn't for the fact that I can't fit into my clothes, it's almost like I never gave birth to him at all."

There was no response I could give that would possibly make her feel better. I felt my heart reach out to this young mother, whose circumstances were so dramatically different from my own, but whose love for her baby was precisely the same. I was suddenly so deeply ashamed of my previous thoughts that her child would be better off in other arms. Who was I to say such a thing?

After a few moments Sandra said, "I should probably tell you what I'm in for."

"Only if you want to."

It was a heroin deal. Sandra had introduced a new friend of hers to her dealer, and the two men had cooked up a scheme to take advantage of the L.A.–Kabul heroin distribution network that had gotten so vigorous since the U.S. invasion. Sandra's new friend, however, turned out to be a confidential informant, working for the cops. For some reason the prosecutors decided to take pity on her and prosecute her in state court rather than federal. Or maybe the feds just wanted to throw the county D.A. a bone. Sandra pled guilty and was sentenced to five years, and was lucky to get it. If she'd been prosecuted in federal court she would have gone to jail for two or three times as long.

One of the things you learn as a public defender is that the line between those who end up in jail and those of us whose lives are untouched by this kind of trouble can be very thin. Sometimes it's a matter of evildoers getting caught, but more often than not it's a question of the fortunes of people's lives, the accidents of fate and birth. Had my parents both died when I was young, as Sandra's had, might I have ended up a heroin addict, caught up in a drug deal, in jail on conspiracy charges? Anything is possible. I was so lucky in my life, and she was so unlucky. My babies were home safe in my beautiful, ramshackle house. Sandra had no idea where hers was. I decided at that moment that I was going to help this young woman, not because of Chiki and his cousin, not because Al and I had little else to do right then, but because I owed it to whatever it was in the world that had allowed me such good fortune and cursed her with such unhappiness.

Right before I left, Sandra said, "If the Lambs of the Lord try to have my parental rights terminated, do you think I could have Noah's birth father come forward and demand custody?"

I had been waiting for Sandra to mention the father and was relieved that I didn't need to bring it up myself. I flipped my notebook to an empty page. "I'm not a family law attorney, but I am absolutely certain that the baby's father is entitled to custody of the child. Unless, of course, there's a reason that he would be denied custody on his own."

"Tweezer's a junkie."

"Is he still using?"

She shrugged. "Probably. I mean, when I'm

with him he can stay clean, more or less. But not on his own."

"I'm not sure, then, that it would help your case to have him come forward." She frowned. "Do you want me to get in touch with him?"

She shook her head. "I don't think so. Not yet. I hear from him sometimes. Or people tell me where he is. We lost our apartment in Eagle Rock after I got arrested, so he's been staying with friends. If I need to find him I'll be able to." Sandra pushed her chair back across the tiles with a decisive squeak and opened the door to the interview room. "I am grateful for your help, Juliet. I wish I could pay you in something more than gratitude, but that's all I have left to offer."

# Eight

BACK out in the parking lot, I plugged the breast pump into the cigarette lighter, turned on the car engine, and did my best to achieve a modicum of discretion by lowering my shirt over the tops of the flanges. I watched a few cars drift in and out of the parking lot and almost nodded off, the rhythmic hum of the motor lulling my chronically sleep-deprived self to sleep. I jerked myself awake and, holding the pump flanges with one hand, I called the office with the other. Al was out, unfortunately, but Chiki was there, waiting for me to check in.

"Damn," I said at the news that my partner was on the shooting range.

"You need some help, Juliet?"

"Yes, but you can't help me. I need Al to do a quick address search."

"Who are you looking for?"

"The social worker at the prison, Taylor Brock. There's no way they're going to let me into the prison to see her without an appointment and permission from the warden. I figured I'd have better luck just showing up at her house." Since Sandra had said the social worker was only at the prison during the morning shift, there was a chance I could find her at home. Now I was going to have to rely on the telephone operator, and the likelihood of Ms. Brock being listed was slim. Individuals who work in law enforcement rarely are. They are less sophisticated, however, at keeping their addresses off the Web.

"436 Peachwood Lane. In Dartmore Village."

"Excuse me?"

"There's a T. Brock at 436 Peachwood Lane."

"Please tell me you did not just use the computer."

"Go on, check your BlackBerry. I bet there's an email from Al with driving directions from Dartmore to 436 Peachwood Lane."

"Did *Al* also turn up an actual office address of

the Lambs of the Lord?" The address I got from Sandra's documents was the same as the one I got from Sister Pauline—a post office box in Pleasanton: their mail drop.

For a moment I heard rapid clicking that sounded suspiciously like tapping on a computer, but that of course must have been something else. A long-toenailed rodent clicking across the cement floor of the office?

"Dang," Chiki said.

"Dang, what?"

"Nothing. I'm just surprised at what a good job the Lambs are doing at hiding their business address. It's, like, nowhere. I can't find it in any of the usual places."

"*You* can't find it?"

"I mean, Al can't find it. Man, whoever they have doing this for them is *good*. You know what? You got to go to Pleasanton today? Because I know I—I mean, Al—can find it. It just might take some doing. It's like trapping a mouse, you know? You come at it from every direction, bit by bit, until you're holding it in your hand."

I looked at the clock on the dashboard of my

rental car. I had just enough time to get over to Taylor Brock's house and grill her before making the drive back to the San Jose airport. As little as I relished the idea, I was going to have to come back up to northern California some other day to visit the office of the Lambs of the Lord. Another flight. Not to mention the hours. This non-case of ours was going to end up costing Al and me more in expenses than most of our actual cases did. And there was no one to reimburse us this time. I glanced over at the hulking prison building behind the razor wire. The money didn't really seem to matter.

"I'm sure if you gave Al some very specific instructions, and a few hours, even he could figure out how to use the computer to track the Lambs down. Chiki, you've got to be careful with what you're up to in the office. You don't want that probation officer of yours barging in while you're doing something you shouldn't be. They make unannounced work and home visits. You know that."

"I'm in a windowless garage with the door locked, Juliet. But don't worry. I won't touch the computer. I won't even breathe on it. How about that? Not even to download you the patches for your system software that were released today. You'll have to figure out how to keep your computer from crashing all on your own."

# Nine

TAYLOR Brock was convinced, I could tell, that she was on the side of the angels. She thought her job was to heal a terrible wrong in the world. The evil she repaired was that which was done to the tender souls of innocent babies, babies forced to spend their lives tied to the wickedness that was their natural mothers. Taylor, through wisdom and luck, was in a position to do something about it. She could take these innocent little lambs and bestow them on loving families, who would raise them as all children deserve to be raised.

It's not like she told me any of this. I'm extrapolating, but I think it would be safe to wager on the accuracy of my conjecture. The woman gave off the unmistakable odor of self-righteousness. She reeked of smug conceit. She was absolutely confident that whatever rules she had technically violated, justice and God were on her side. She felt no fear of my condemnation. It amused her.

I found Ms. Brock in her garden, deadheading roses with a sharp and cruel-looking pair of pruning shears. The rose bushes were trained like topiary, their twisted stems rising like miniature tree trunks about three feet off the ground, and the tops cropped in perfect globes of leaves and blooms. They alternated red, white, and pink. Ms. Brock's own figure was similarly trained, forced by dint of hardworking undergarments into a tubular shape. Her hair was its own series of steel-gray tubes, one upon the other, and I could just tell she had it set weekly by a hairdresser who still believed in the magical powers of Dippity-Do.

The garden was protected by a low picket fence, white of course. I parked my car and, standing on the street side of the garden, called out to Ms. Brock. She snipped the heads off two overblown roses, caught them in her flowered glove, and laid them in her basket before responding to my greeting. I made my business clear; I told her that I was there to inquire after her role in soliciting pregnant prisoners for the Lambs of the Lord. I had hoped to take her by surprise, to put her on the defensive.

She rocked back on the heels of her gardening clogs—yellow, with ladybugs—and said, "And the Lord Jesus said, 'Suffer the little children to come unto Me, and forbid them not: for of such is the Kingdom of God.' Mark, chapter 10, verse 14." Then she snapped the air with her clippers, as if to punctuate the Bible verse.

"Ms. Brock," I began.

"Miss."

"Excuse me?"

"Miss. I am not a feminist. I prefer Miss."

I moved closer so that I was standing right next to the fence. "Miss Brock. Both Sister Pauline Hubblebank and Sandra Lorgeree would like their little children to come unto *them.* Or, in Sandra's case, unto her family. She's asked me to find her child, and I think you can help me."

Miss Brock shook her head, an expression of sad tolerance on her face. "I can see that you're a person who really cares for my Dartmore girls," she said.

*My* Dartmore girls? What did that mean?

"Yes, I do care."

"As I've told all my girls at Dartmore, their problem is that they seek the wrong thing. Instead of looking for children whose lives can only be improved by their mothers' absences, these girls should seek salvation in the Lord's embrace. For as Jesus said, 'You will seek me and find me when you seek me with all your heart.' Jeremiah, chapter 29, I believe. Although I might be wrong. My memory for numbers does fail me at times."

"Miss Brock, that's hardly your decision to make, is it? As the social worker charged with the task of helping the women at the facility deal with issues such as guardianship and foster care, I assume your ethical obligation is to the women, correct? To your clients?"

"My obligation is clear to me," she said. "Therefore to Him that knoweth to do good, and doeth it not, to Him it is sin."

This placid and self-satisfied scripture quoting was going to make me leap the fence and strangle the woman. I gripped the posts with my hands and did my best to control myself. "Miss Brock, I can think of a dozen federal statutes you've violated by encouraging the Dartmore prisoners to hand over their infants to the Lambs of the Lord when you know full well that at least some of those babies are not going to be returned."

She sighed, as if disappointed at the implied threat of my words. "What is at stake is so much greater," she said. " 'Whosoever shall not receive the Kingdom of God as a little child shall in no wise enter therein.' Luke, chapter 18, verse 17. You tell Sister Pauline that I wish her well, and that her little girl's soul is saved." She snipped a rose, tossed it into her basket, and then, without another word, stalked up the path to her front door, leaving me fuming in her wake, clutching the fence.

After a moment or two my cell phone rang. Chiki said, "I've got a street address for the Lambs. I don't know if it's any good, but it's a Pleasanton address. You want it?"

"I'll get the address tomorrow. I can't make it to Pleasanton today. I've got to get home to my kids."

# Ten

PETER had spent the day ignoring the children. When I got home that evening, I found Ruby and Isaac lying in the family room watching a video, on either side of a pizza box containing an uneaten, congealing pizza. The baby was hanging off Peter's chest, and by the state of the Baby Bjorn—trails of white spit-up stains, leg openings mysteriously dampened, straps twisted—she'd been there for a long time. All day, perhaps. Peter had his telephone headset on and was pacing back and forth, his normally cheerful expression replaced by a torqued and twisted mask of anxiety so intense it was almost comical.

"Hi," I said.

When Sadie heard my voice she let loose with a series of high-pitched wails. I undid her disgusting harness, letting the top fall against Peter's thighs. He continued his frenzied pacing, now with the Baby Bjorn flopping along his front like a filthy apron.

"Daddy's a crazy person," I whispered into Sadie's ear. She snuffled, rooting around in my shirt. I sat down on the floor next to Ruby and Isaac. "Hi, Mom," I said. "We missed you so much. Gee, that's nice, kids. I missed you, too. How was your day, Mom? Fine, how was yours?"

Isaac pried himself loose from *Rugrats*. "Hi, Mom," he said.

"Hi, baby."

"It's Parent Appreciation Breakfast next week at school."

"I know. Daddy and I are planning to be there."

"Oh," he said. His eyes drifted back to the television. "I don't think the scones will taste very good. Flora Stein-McPhee has a cold and she sneezed into the dough a lot today. A whole lot."

"Really?"

"Yeah. Booger scones."

"Gross."

"Totally gross. You're probably going to think they're raisins. But they're boogers."

"I'll try not to be fooled. The scones will be pretty stale if you guys were making them today, anyway."

"Bracha and Sue are gonna *freeze* them, Mom." He shook his head at my ignorance.

I prodded his sister's behind with my toe. "Hey Rubes. How long has Daddy been on the phone?"

She shrugged.

"Who's he talking to?"

She shrugged again.

"Wake up, Ruby!" I said sternly.

She rolled her eyes and turned to look at me, ostentatiously staring me right in the face.

"Who is Daddy talking to?"

"I don't know." Her enunciation was over-correct, as if she were talking to an elderly foreign tourist who was a touch deaf. "His lawyer, he said."

I looked over at Peter. As far as I knew, he didn't have a lawyer. He had an agent, and his agent had a lawyer who looked over Peter's contracts to make sure he hadn't agreed to serve up our firstborn to the movie studio in exchange for gross points, but as far as I knew the only lawyer my husband had ever *had* was me, and he wasn't getting much of me lately. Ha ha.

"Honey?" I called out.

Peter flicked his hand at me in the universal "Leave me alone, I'm talking on the phone" gesture. The one specifically designed to piss off your wife.

"Peter! Who are you talking to?"

"Hold on a second, okay?" he said into the receiver. Then he covered it with his hand. "I'm on a conference call with the guy from the studio legal department and with the rest of our litigation team."

"Your *litigation team*?"

"Yeah. As soon as the studio was served they called in the team. We're strategizing our defense."

"*You're* strategizing the defense?"

He shrugged. "Mostly I'm doing a lot of swearing. But that seems to be an important part of the litigation process. At least the lawyers all seem to appreciate it."

"I'll bet. Are you going to be done anytime soon?"

"I don't know. They're conferencing in some exec from features. Apparently, he's the bozo who took a meeting with the clown. He's going to get his head on a platter, I can tell you that. Wait a second, they're back." He returned to his call and resumed his assigned task.

Rather than have my children add to their already colorful vocabularies, I hustled them into the bath. Ruby held Sadie on her lap as I shampooed everybody's hair and soaped them clean. I like the three of them best when they are all together in one bathtub, confined to a small space, all fragrant and warm. Sadie loves the tub, and her giggling is contagious. The three of them laughed and wriggled, their soft skin covered with bubbles, their wet hair plastered to their cheeks, their eyes glowing in the bright light reflected off the white tiles. Their bathroom, like all five in the house—it seems Mr. Navarro had a thing for cleanliness—was furnished with a massive claw-foot tub. We'd allowed them to choose which bathroom they wanted for their own, and it had been an immediate and unanimous decision. Theirs was the dragon bathroom. The walls were papered in a kind of rubberized, metallic crimson, and all the fixtures were of golden dragons, including the taps and spouts. The kids looked like magical little nymphs, cavorting under the protective eye of a dozen ruby-eyed reptile kings. God only knows what the bathroom's previous occupants had gotten up to in there.

By the time I bundled Ruby and Isaac into bed, read them *A Day with Wilbur Robinson* and *The Leaf Man,* and nursed Sadie to sleep, Peter had finally finished his conference call and was sucking down a St. Pauli Girl like it was his last drink before rehab. And he doesn't even like beer.

"That was some conversation," I said. "Were you on the phone all day?"

He shook his head and said defensively, "It was hardly all day. And it wasn't like it was one long call. We talked a few times during the day. This is serious, Juliet."

"It's a frivolous case filed by a nutcase. I'll bet the studio attorneys deal with this kind of thing every week."

"Well, this particular nutcase has managed to find himself counsel. Very aggressive counsel."

"I'm sure it will be all right."

For a few minutes we had a ridiculous argument during which Peter tried to convince me that it would *not* be all right and I tried to belittle his hysteria. Neither of us could acknowledge the underlying truth about the argument. I would not admit to being dismissive, and Peter would not concede that his feelings were hurt. We'd had this fight so many times before, but I was the one who usually had the hurt feelings and Peter was the one who was usually guilty of claiming everything was fine.

Finally Peter said, "You're so busy fighting with me that you didn't even let me tell you the most ridiculous part. You'll never believe what this guy does, in addition to taking meetings in Hollywood and not getting his pitches produced."

"What does he do?"

"He owns a crafts store."

"He does not."

"He does. In Calabasas. On Valley Circle Boulevard. I found it on the Web. He has a big mail order business, apparently. His specialty is macramé."

"No way! I was just up there, in Canoga Park. I could have stopped in and picked up a few God's Eyes. Or a skein of alpaca wool."

"Or you could have beaten him up for me."

I was immediately sorry for bickering with him. Peter knows that all he has to do to defuse my irritation is appeal to my protective impulses. He has on occasion referred to me, in very loving tones, as his own personal pit bull. I sat down on the couch and pulled his feet into my lap. I rubbed them, concentrating on his high arches. Peter has lovely feet, beautifully constructed, with flat, even nails, round heels, and sharply indented ankles. Before I met him I used to cringe in preparation for seeing a boyfriend's feet for the first time. Invariably, there would be some horror lurking under those innocuous argyles. A hammertoe with a gnarled, black nail. Skinny, mismatched toes that overlapped. Or, worst of all, long toenails. There is nothing as deadening to the mood as the sight of ten ragged and filthy toenails curling over the tops of a handsome man's ugly feet. It's enough to make a woman swear off sex forever. But Peter's toes are lovely. He could have an alternative career as a foot model. The first time I saw his bare feet I had thrown him onto my bed and not let him up for days. Tonight, alas, I evinced as much sex drive as if I'd pulled off his sweat socks to reveal a scary, stinky, normal boy's foot. That is to say, none at all.

"How was your day?" he asked. "Did you get any closer to finding out where that woman's baby is?"

I shook my head. "No. No closer."

"Will you, do you think?"

"God, I hope so. Although, what's going to happen then? Sandra's in jail. She can't keep the baby.

And she has no idea where her family is. She hasn't seen them in years. We'll probably be able to help her track them down, but who's to say they'll want the baby if we find him. Or if they do, that they'll be competent to care for him. It's just such a mess."

Peter wriggled his toes, stretched, and said, "That sounds like a terrible situation. Are you sure you want to be involved?"

"I don't have a choice."

"Why not? Why don't you have a choice? It's not like she's really a client."

"She is *so* a client. Just because she can't pay me doesn't mean I don't owe her an ethical obligation. And I don't have a choice, because she doesn't have anyone else. I'm all she's got. I have to help her."

Peter opened his mouth, as if to object, but then closed it again. He sighed and said, "I'd better go down to my office and get something done tonight. The last thing I want to do is let Macramé Man distract me from my work."

I took the copy of my book club book to bed with me, but I just couldn't motivate myself to read. It was hard to keep turning the pages when I knew the fate that John Updike had in store for the main character. Finally, I gave in to my baser impulses and pulled my laptop out from under the bed, where I kept it for just such nocturnal emergencies. Peter hadn't managed to fix the leaking faucets or get our bedroom door to close properly, but he had installed a wireless connection throughout the house. With Sadie snoring softly in bed next to me, I Googled Taylor Brock, grateful that her name was unusual enough to have generated only four hundred or so hits. It took me just a few minutes to figure out why Miss Brock seemed so sanguine, so assured of her impunity. Among the various records of her employment, her graduation with a master's degree in social work from Cal State Hayward, and her church-affiliated activities, I found a newspaper profile that included a reference to Miss Brock. The subject of the profile was her brother, Franklin Brock, the executive vice president of the California Correctional Peace Officers Association. Miss Brock wasn't afraid for her job, despite her unethical and perhaps even illegal activities, because she knew that the very force that controlled the California prisons, if not the whole state, protected her. Her brother was one of the men in charge of the prison guards' union. For years the union has dominated Sacramento, using their financial clout to elect and destroy politicians according to their own narrow agenda. It's the guards, not the administrators, who run the prisons nowadays. Squirrelly legislators with their eyes on their pocketbooks have ensured that. Goon squads that take down any elected official standing in their way guarantee it. No wonder Taylor Brock's only response to our confrontation was to quote scripture and walk away.

It was a long, sleepless night for me. I was awake when Sadie woke for her midnight feed, and I was awake when Peter came to bed at three. I was beside myself with exhaustion by morning, and in no mood for Isaac's complicated frame of mind.

"Where's your lunch box?" I asked him. I was holding his hastily assembled lunch, or what passed for lunch given that I hadn't gone grocery shopping in a week and that his preschool had officially banned anything with peanuts in it. I'm not a cruel person; I understand and sympathize with the tribulations of children with food allergies. But I cannot believe that school officials appreciate the true ramifications of the peanut butter ban. What are those of us with less than Martha Stewart–like homemaking skills supposed to slap between two pieces of bread when we forget to go to the grocery store? Peanut butter I could buy at Costco in ten-gallon drums. Try that with turkey breast.

"It's in my backpack."

"Well, go get it."

Isaac dumped the backpack on the floor next to me. I gritted my teeth. Would it have killed him to place it in my outstretched hand? In the backpack I found his lunch box and a juice box, opened, its contents spilled all over the rest of the backpack's contents.

"Isaac! You put an open juice box into your backpack!"

He blinked at me, slack-jawed.

"Isaac!"

"What?"

"You can't put an open juice box into your backpack! Look, you got your backpack all wet, and you ruined all your papers." I shook out the soaked drawings, most of which looked like Isaac had stumbled across them holding a marker in his outstretched hand. At least I could not be blamed for shoving these in the trash. Or so I thought.

"You're throwing away my pictures!"

"They're wet."

His lower lip pushed out and his eyes filled with tears. "My pictures," he murmured, as though he'd worked for all four years of his life on these crumpled artistic efforts.

"Make me new ones today, okay?"

He lifted his narrow shoulders helplessly, as if even contemplating that was too much for him.

"What's this?" I said, holding up a sheet of paper. I scanned it quickly. "It's a note about the Parent Appreciation Breakfast."

"You shouldn't come, because the scones are all boogery, remember? And the coffee will be from Peet's. You hate Peet's coffee, you say it's too strong."

"Daddy loves Peet's coffee. And I'll have tea. We'll be there, don't worry."

"You don't have to come."

"Of course we'll come. Don't worry, Isaac."

He sighed dramatically and took a small, sad bite of toast.

I picked Sadie up from her bouncy seat and put her on the breast to top her off before we set out on our car pool rounds. Even on good days, when I've had more than a couple of hours' sleep, I hate to stop in the middle of car pool to nurse the baby. Today, when I was so tired, having to pull over for a mid-flight refueling would be a disaster. Nursing always makes me sleepy, and I'd probably end up napping on the side of Beverly Boulevard. Not a good way to start the day.

The telephone rang while I was struggling to get Sadie to latch on and I almost let the machine pick it up. I might have, but Ruby got there before me.

"Wyeth-Applebaum residence, this is Ruby speaking." She frowned. "Mama, someone wants to know if we accept collect calls from Dartmore Prison."

"Yes!" I said. "Always, Ruby. We always accept collect calls from prisons."

"Yes," she said into the phone. "We like getting collect calls from prisons."

I held out my hand. "Give me the phone."

"This is Ruby, can I help you?"

"Give me the phone, Ruby."

"She's right here, but she's nursing Sadie."

"Ruby! Give me the phone this instant!"

"Can she call you back?"

"Ruby, if you don't hand me that phone I'm going to give you a spanking!"

She rolled her eyes and handed over the receiver.

My daughter, alas, knows just how realistic my threats of corporal punishment are.

"Hello, this is Juliet," I said.

"This is Fidelia, Chiki's cousin."

I could tell right away that something was terribly wrong. Fidelia sounded crushed, her voice tiny and lifeless.

"What happened?"

"Sandra's dead. She was killed last night."

This was not the first time I'd gotten news like this over the telephone, nor even the first time I'd gotten news like this from a prisoner. Each time I had been nothing short of devastated, wrenched by the reminder of the terrible danger of prison, of the lawlessness and violence governing the lives of people inside. This time, however, seemed somehow worse than the others. Perhaps because Sandra was a woman, perhaps because she was a new mother, perhaps because I'd seen her so recently. This time the tragic waste struck me with a terrible force, and it took some moments for me to catch my breath.

"I'm so sorry, Fidelia," I said, my voice cracking.

Fidelia sobbed suddenly, as if my sympathy had triggered a breakdown in her control. If we had been sitting close together I would have put my arm around her, held her hand, offered some physical comfort. The murmurs I could give over the telephone wire were entirely insufficient.

"What happened?" I asked when her cries had ebbed.

"A shiv, out on the yard," she said. "I didn't see it but they're saying . . ." she paused. "I don't believe what they're saying. Even when she wanted to change bunkies, she was careful about how she did it. And since then she's been real good to everyone, helping them with their legal cases and all. I don't believe it's true, what they're saying."

I knew that that was as much as Fidelia could tell me. Even if there were no prisoners standing nearby who could hear her, all telephone conversations going in and out of the prison were recorded, and Fidelia was savvy enough to watch her words, especially since the sister of one of the leaders of the guards' union was no friend of Sandra's.

"Find her baby, Juliet. Please find Noah. Maybe you think now it doesn't matter, because she's dead, but it does. It does matter, more than ever. I've got to make sure you find him, for Sandra's sake."

"I will, Fidelia. I promise."

# *Eleven*

WHEN Al wrapped himself in his Los Angeles cop persona, I could almost see his uniform, hovering like a dark blue ghost around his seated figure. He had someone from the warden's office at Dartmore on speakerphone, and after introducing himself as "Detective Al Hockey, from down in L.A.," Al spent some time replying to the man's questions about precincts, with references to the ones he worked in more than ten years ago. Needless to say, he did not mention the time lag. Within a few minutes he had moved beyond the LAPD and was playing U.S. Army geography with the man on the other end of the line. ("I can always tell when I'm talking to a military man.") They both, it turned out, were with the 101st Airborne at more or less the same time and couldn't quite believe they hadn't met up in Cam Ranh Bay or the Song Con Valley.

Fifteen minutes later we had our information. Sandra Lorgeree was killed, said the deputy warden, in a hit ordered by the Aryan Brotherhood.

"The gang's women's auxiliary, you could say," the deputy said. "We don't know who did the hit. The witnesses were only willing to say that the killer had the tattoo—a little picture of a girl in combat boots with a baseball bat. They all have it, all the Aryan Women."

I wrote the word "hit" followed by a doubtful question mark.

"What makes you think it was a hit?" Al said.

"All the markings. Yard stabbing. No witnesses. Right through the thorax, so the killer knew what she was doing. We don't get that a lot around here, not like in the men's facilities. Fights, sure, even stabbings, but not a clean hit like this. Not someone dead in the yard and no one willing to say much. It's got to be the Brotherhood. No other explanation."

"Any idea why?" Al said. "The victim was a white girl, wasn't she?"

"She had some problems with the Aryan Women when she first got here. Ended up in the SHU over it. I'm guessing it took a while for the order to come down from the men's prison. They don't do much without being told, the Aryan Women. What we're figuring is that they sent their complaint on up to the men, and then they got authorization for the hit."

Al thanked his source and hung up the phone. He looked at me over the top of his reading glasses. "You buy it?" he said.

"No."

"Me neither."

"Why would they need *authorization* to kill someone?"

Al shook his head. "I'm guessing if they wanted her dead, it would have happened months ago."

"Exactly," I said. "Not that I would put it past the those fascists to order a hit. And if they did, there's no way the women would talk. No one would snitch on the Aryan Brotherhood. But there's just not a good enough reason for them to order a hit."

Al took off his glasses and chewed thoughtfully on the end. "Unless . . ." he began.

"Unless they were paid. They work for hire, the Brand does. Not just for ideology."

"Bingo."

The Aryan Brotherhood, or the Brand, as it is commonly known, is a white-supremacist gang that has effectively taken over many prisons, especially the maximum-security facilities. They engage in drug trafficking, prostitution, and extortion, all within the prison walls. They also murder, often seemingly with impunity. After all, when someone is serving two life terms on twenty-three-hour-a-day lockdown in a Supermax, what can he possibly have to lose? Members of the Brand kill all kinds of people: some just because they don't like them—they hate African Americans, homosexuals, child molesters, informants, prison guards, and Jews—and some because they've been paid to do so. Murder for hire is a lucrative business in the prison system. Sometimes a prisoner will commit murder in return for a few thousand dollars delivered to a wife or girlfriend on the outside, sometimes for a few grams of heroin delivered to a cell. Sometimes for the services of a particularly attractive or youthful companion.

"I hate those scumbags," Al said. He slowly drew his hands into fists, cracking the knuckles, as if imagining what he would do to the men who would consider his contented marriage an obscenity and his beautiful daughters mongrels.

"You and me both," I said. "But you know, Al, nowadays, these guys aren't even about ideology. There are guys inside with the shamrock tattoo who couldn't care less about killing Jews or blacks. It's a gang—it's about crime and power."

"I still hate them."

"Yeah, so do I," I said.

"And a woman. They got a woman to stab her."

I knew what he meant. It never fails to surprise me when we come across women who are as cruel, as violent, as their male counterparts. By and large, women's prisons are less horrific places than men's, exploitation movies like *Slammer Girls* and *Caged Heat* notwithstanding. There is violence, sure, even sexual violence, but most often it comes at the hands of the guards. The misery of incarceration for women is not usually about fear of their fellow prisoners. The misery comes from terrible living conditions, separation from children and family, woefully inadequate medical care, and mistreatment by those in power.

Our clients at the federal defender's office were overwhelmingly male. When, every once in a while,

I represented a woman, it was most often someone who had been lured into the criminal enterprise through a boyfriend or husband. The worst crime committed by most of the women I represented was having bad taste in men. There were, of course, violent women, although generally I didn't see them in my practice. As a federal public defender, my caseload consisted of drug cases, bank robberies, the odd white-collar crime. I did not, by and large, defend individuals accused of crimes like assault or murder, except in the context of a drug transaction, or if the crime occurred on federal property. Still, even in state court, women who stood accused of violent crime most often had as their victims abusive husbands or lovers.

The woman who killed Sandra Lorgeree, whether she'd committed the murder out of racist rage, personal animosity, or for financial gain, was either an unusual and frightening creature or so under the thumb of the men of the Brand that they'd turned her into one.

It helped that Al and I were not busy with other work, but I think that even if our office had been groaning under the weight of cases, we both would still have devoted our time to Sandra and her baby.

Neither of us could stomach the idea of stopping, of giving up. It would have meant giving in to what had befallen Sandra, and we were both too stubborn to do that. We don't have very much in common, my partner and I, but one thing we share is a mule-headed stubbornness. This quality is one that we admire tremendously in each other. We're lucky in this, because everyone else in our lives finds it excessively irritating.

"I'll go to Pleasanton with you," Al said.

"Just give me a couple of days to stockpile enough breast-milk to see Sadie through another day without me."

Poor Sadie. There is a photo album chronicling every month of Ruby's first year. Even Isaac had managed to fill three albums by his first birthday, and at least half a dozen of the pictures in there were of him alone, without his sister. Other than the official hospital photograph marking Sadie's birth, and a few shots of her older siblings holding her in their laps, Sadie's first months had gone by entirely unremarked upon—at least on photo stock. I had made her no baby book, and had I managed to motivate myself to do so, instead of the requisite notations of the first smile, first tooth, and lock of hair from the first trim, it would have been far more honest to make an inventory of the indignities she suffered that her siblings never had. Being separated from her mother at the age of four months, from dawn until dusk twice in a single week, probably wouldn't have ended up high on the list.

# Twelve

AL and I did not premeditate our masquerade. Our intention when we left John Wayne Airport in Orange County (the only airport Al consents to fly out of—he says because it's smaller and better managed; I think it's because he fancies himself a lot like the Duke) was to do a simple interview. Our plans remained the same when we landed in Oakland, when we squeezed ourselves into the miniature doors of the Monopoly playing piece the rental car agency insisted on referring to as a "car," and all the way along the freeway winding through the gray-green hills to Pleasanton. It was only when we entered the offices of the Lambs of the Lord that

our mendacious plan began to hatch. Its birth occurred simultaneously in both our minds.

I took one look at the artfully framed portrait of
the young blond couple, their cheeks painted in rosy
tones, their eyes the blue of the sapphire seas, and I
knew what we needed to do. I nodded toward the
painting with just the barest motion of my head, and
Al took in with a glance the dark-haired baby the
couple held, its skin dusky gold, its eyes a muddy
color somewhere between brown and black. Over
the trio hovered an angel with palms outstretched in
benediction. Al aimed a nearly invisible wink back
at me.

"Welcome to the Lambs of the Lord," a smiling
older woman said. She sat behind a reception desk
that was new but made to look antique, with elaborate scrollwork and spindle legs. The sleek, black,
multi-line telephone looked incongruous in the
middle of the polished cherry expanse. The lines all
blinked, but the receptionist ignored them. "Can I
help you?"

"We don't have an appointment, I'm afraid. But
we're interested in applying to be foster parents." I
could not believe I had allowed that faux-Southern
twang to creep into my voice. Now I was going to

have to keep it up for the entire visit, otherwise the Lambs would think I was insane. Yet another reason why one-time high school thespians should avoid undercover work.

"Oh, that's all right," she said. "You can go ahead and fill out a fostering application. Mr. Summer has some time this morning. That's Joe Summer, our executive director. I can probably talk him into conducting an interview."

"Y'all are so kind," I said. "Do y'all need to see some form of identification?" I began rummaging in my purse.

"Oh, no. That's all right. Just fill out the paperwork. After your interview I'll have to get your fingerprints, but that's just a formality. And don't you worry, we've got this printing pad with invisible ink. No nasty black stuff to stain that pretty sweater of yours."

Al and I sat in adjoining chairs and wordlessly began creating a fictitious life as a couple. He knocked ten years off his age, and I added five to mine, putting us close enough to make our marriage believable. Sadie had kept me up the night before, so I was exhausted enough to look Al's real age, let alone my pretend one. The job Al wrote down for himself was the one he always gives when assuming a fake identity: assistant manager of a direct mail processing facility. Very occasionally, when he needs more authority, he becomes the manager. The idea behind the identity is that it is believable while at the same time so tedious that it elicits absolutely no questions. Al has even learned a few bits of direct mail lingo—phrases like "lift letters" and "freemiums"—enough to lend credibility yet scare away even the hardiest conversationalist.

I wrote down that I was a homemaker. That was not far from the truth. While I was a part-time investigator, most of my time was spent with my children, although hardly at home. Today's stay-at-home mother does anything but. A better descriptive phrase would somehow incorporate the real heart of the modern family. I was a stay-in-minivan-mom. A station-wagon-maker.

It took a long time to fill out the detailed questionnaire about our income ($42,000 per year), our home (Al's in Westminster), our family backgrounds (Los Angeles born and bred), our religious affiliation (Covenant Pentecostal Church in Westminster—a mile or so from Al's house and an island of white, evangelical prayer in an otherwise multicultural city). By the time we were done, I felt like I knew Al and Juliet Cromley (another familiar alias—one we both used) quite well. I didn't like them much.

Mr. Summer, however, had different taste. He liked them an awful lot. So much, in fact, that within fifteen minutes he was behaving as though he were the one being interviewed, so eager was he that we agree to become foster parents for his agency. He extolled the social value of taking care of at-risk children. He called them "little lost souls" and talked movingly of the satisfaction of watching a child with no advantages, a "flower from the rockiest soil," blossom and flourish under loving and competent care. His words were compelling, and I had to remind myself that some of these souls were not, in fact, "lost" at all. They had family members ready and able to care for them, and their own mothers wanted them. What Mr. Summer thought of the quality of the care offered by these mothers was only too obvious.

"I do have one question," I asked when he seemed to be winding down.

"What's that, Juliet? May I call you that?"

"Of course you may. I was just wondering what

happens when the girls get out of jail. I mean, my husband and I, we're affectionate folks, and we've been waiting on a baby for a long time now." I was really getting into my down-home, country drawl. "It would just about break our hearts if the mother got out of jail and came looking for her baby."

Mr. Summer leaned conspiratorially across the table. "Juliet, let me say this. The job of the Lambs of the Lord, my job, is to place a baby with you, in your home. What happens after that, that's out of our control."

"But . . ."

"Wait, let me finish," he said. "If, say, you move and we don't have your address, then there's no way we can track you or the baby down. Especially if you move out of state. It gets very difficult in those circumstances. In fact, we've never been able to find a couple who didn't want to be found."

Al said, "So what you're telling us is that you'll give us a baby, and if we move away with it, then that's our business, whether the natural mother comes looking or not?"

Mr. Summer leaned back in his chair. "In a manner of speaking."

"So we'd get to keep our baby?" I said.

He smiled. "If we couldn't track you down, then you would of course keep your baby. We can only do so much at the Lambs of the Lord. We're a foster care agency, not a detective agency."

Al looked at me and I nodded.

"That's very interesting, Joe," Al said. "Because Juliet and I actually *are* a detective agency. You don't mind if I call you Joe, do you?"

The blood left the man's face, leaving it ashen.

"We're here on behalf of one of those natural mothers," I said, dropping the accent. "One of the women whose babies you aren't able or interested in tracking down once you've placed them."

"You can't prove anything," he said. "I didn't say anything. It's your word against mine."

I reached into my capacious handbag and took out my microcassette recorder. "Your words and ours are all on tape, Joe. Al, can you count how many state and federal crimes Mr. Summer has broken with this baby-stealing ring of his?"

"Well, there's accessory to kidnapping, for one," Al said. "And fraud, those are the easy ones."

"What do you want?" Joe said, his face contorted in anxiety. "What do you want from me?"

"We want Sandra Lorgeree's baby," I said.

"Who?"

"Sandra Lorgeree. A prisoner at Dartmore. Her son Noah was born two months ago. Who did you place him with? I want the name, address, driver's license numbers, Social Security numbers, everything you have on the couple."

"We never fostered a child born to any Sandra Lorgeree."

"Yes, you did."

"No, we didn't."

"Yes, you did."

"Look, I'll show you," he said. With a few strokes on his keyboard he brought up a database on his computer screen. "The paper files are organized by the last name of the fostering family, but we can search the computer records using anything, including the birth mother's name." He input Sandra's name, asking me to spell Lorgeree. The screen flashed "No Records Match Inquiry."

"Put in Hubblebank—Pauline," I said.

"I know that name's here," he said. "It's a small agency; we've only fostered two dozen children. I recognize that name."

"Input it," I said.

He did, using the same process he had for Sandra's name. Pauline's daughter's file immediately came up on the screen. Her name was no longer Taniel Hubblebank, however. It was listed as Samantha Krause, and she lived in Danville, California, with her parents Barbara and Philip.

"You didn't arrange for a foster family for Sandra's baby?" I said.

"No."

"And you're willing to stake me taking this tape to the FBI, the Department of Social Services, and the newspapers, on your word?"

"That baby was never in our custody."

"Well, do you know whose custody he *was* in?"

"No."

Al and I both looked at Joe Summer, sizing up his veracity.

Suddenly I thought of something. "Do you have a packet of information you give to the mothers?"

"Excuse me?"

"The prisoners. Like a brochure and a contract? You must have some documents they sign."

"Of course we do."

"May I see them?"

He looked at me suspiciously, but then handed me a three-fold brochure on cheap, slick paper. The print was off-center, and I noticed a spelling mistake right away. The contract was printed on tissue-thin paper with pale blue ink. These documents could not be more different from the fine engraved stationery Sandra had been sent.

"I don't know anything about that woman or her baby," Joe Summer said. "What will it take for me to get that tape from you?"

I thought of Sister Pauline's daughter, seven months old. I considered my own children at the same age. Attached to me, true, but still so small, so malleable. Memories still undeveloped. I made a decision.

"I want Taniel Hubblebank—the baby you know as Samantha Krause—back in her mother's arms. You do that and you'll get this tape."

"But parental rights have already been terminated in that case."

"Consult an attorney. I'm sure you can figure something out. The court will reopen the case if they are made aware of the fraud. But I'm confident there's an easier way out of this for you."

We left Joe Summer looking battered and his receptionist confused. When we got into the car I said,

"So, what do you think the guy's going to think if he ever gets his hands on this microcassette?"

"I think he's probably going to feel like a jerk for allowing himself to be blackmailed by someone who can't even remember to turn on her tape recorder."

# Thirteen

I pulled on to the freeway, intending to head back to the Oakland Airport, but at the last minute I changed my mind and went south, toward Dartmore.

"Is this okay with you?" I asked Al.

"I suppose so," he said. "Don't have much else to do. Are we going to the prison?"

"No, the hospital."

He shrugged noncommittally and settled back in his chair for a snooze. Al prefers to sleep when I drive. He says that otherwise he wears out his brake foot. His complaints are just payback for my own. I'm always bitching and moaning about how he still drives like he's got a siren on his roof and a badge in his wallet.

The county hospital outside of Dartmore was small, what you'd expect from a rural hospital in a depressed area where by far the largest employers are the prison and a few factory farms. I couldn't help but wonder about the quality of the medicine practiced inside. What kind of physician chooses exile to such a place? Is this really where you'd want to be treated if you were crushed under the wheels of a combine or stabbed in the back with a knife carved from a toothbrush? Not that either population has any choice in the matter.

The hospital comprised two squat buildings linked by a covered walkway. One building was covered in pebbled stucco, the kind sprayed from a hose, and the other building was wrapped in some kind of pale blue rubberized siding. Neither had an obvious main entrance, so I parked more or less in the middle of the lot.

"Do me a favor," I said to Al. "Wander around or something. Kill time in the cafeteria. I'm going to chat up the labor and delivery nurses."

He nodded. Regular folks, especially women,

are always my turf. Al's a terrific investigator, but his interrogation techniques are those taught by the LAPD, and cops are getting busted for that kind of thing nowadays. Our partnership works well if he and his naturally suspicious self do other kinds of legwork. That is, unless confrontation is specifically called for. He's terrific at that. It's funny, because Al's great undercover. It's just that when he's not pretending, he becomes far too gruff and intimidating.

I found my way to Labor and Delivery. It was an entirely different world from the one in which I had my babies. At Cedars-Sinai, the unit was always busy, the private rooms full of laboring and recovering women, nurses bustling about, patients in wheelchairs being whisked to and fro, women walking the halls trailing IV poles, doctors rushing from room to room to catch the last few minutes of drama. If there was someone in labor on this floor, she was having a very quiet delivery. Three women were at the semicircular nurses' station, two wearing pale pink scrubs. A third, in scrubs of traditional green, sat up on the counter, one white-clogged foot resting on a chair.

"Hi," I said.

They greeted me politely.

"I was hoping one of you might be able to help me out with something. A young woman gave birth here two months ago. Sandra Lorgeree. From CCI Dartmore. I'm looking to talk to anyone who might have attended her during or after her labor."

The nurses in the pink scrubs glanced at each other. "Sorry," one said. "We have an awful lot of births. We could never remember one of them in particular."

The four of us gazed around the empty floor and she had the grace to blush.

The other then said, "We can't talk to you about a patient. All that information's confidential."

"Sandra Lorgeree was murdered a few days ago at Dartmore Prison. Before she was killed she asked me to help find the newborn son who was stolen from her." My specific intention was to shock them. I wanted them to go pale with horror. Their response was exactly what I had hoped for.

"Can you help me?" I said.

The three looked at each other. Suddenly, the woman in the green scrubs said in a strangled voice,

"I need some air. Call me if anything comes up. I've got my pager." She leapt down from her perch and rushed to the elevator bank.

I said to the other two, "Please. Won't you help me find this poor woman's baby?"

"We can't," one of the nurses said. "We just can't."

I shook my head, turned, and left. When I turned into the elevator bank I saw the third woman standing in the middle elevator, holding it open for me. She put her finger to her lips and motioned me inside.

"I'm Lois Curtin," she said when the doors had closed. "I'm the midwife who delivered Sandra's baby. We need to talk."

Al noticed us walk into the cafeteria, but made no attempt to come over to the table in the far corner of the room where Lois and I sat.

"I'm not surprised you're here," Lois said. "At least, I'm not surprised *someone's* here. What's going on with these poor women is terrible." The midwife was a woman in her late forties, with short ash-blonde hair cut in an old-fashioned style, a lot like the wedge cut I had sported in junior high school, when I was emulating Dorothy Hamill, before I went into my Farrah Fawcett phase. Her face was lightly lined, especially around the eyes and next to her mouth. She wore the traces of a lifetime of ready smiles.

"You know about the babies being taken?" I said.

She wrapped her strong hands around the Styrofoam cup of coffee she had poured herself before we sat down. "Yes," she said. "That, and all the rest of it."

I knit my brow in confusion. "The rest of it?"

"Animals wouldn't be treated the way those women are. They bring them in here shackled, with their ankles and wrists in chains. By the time they're admitted most of them have been laboring for hours like that. Have you ever been in labor? Can you imagine what it's like to go through that in chains?"

I stared at her, stunned, and remained silent.

"Once the women are in my care, I try to force the guards to unlock them, but most of the time they won't. The guard chains them to the bed by a wrist and a leg. The leg iron stays on until they are ready to push. I can't do anything about the shackles, even if I'd prefer they walk or move."

"That's just despicable," I said. "We're not talking murderers here. The vast majority of those women are in for drug possession or prostitution. Why would the guards think they were a danger? Or are the guards afraid the women are going to try to escape?"

"As if any woman in the throes of labor could manage to escape."

I couldn't bring myself to drink my coffee. "This is just horrifying," I said.

"It gets worse," Lois replied. "I always make sure the nurses provide the prisoners with extra packages of sanitary napkins when they leave the hospital, as well as the disposable undergarments we use. Well, I found out recently that the guards take the supplies away from the women as soon as they get to the prison. The guards then dole them out as they see fit. A woman with postpartum bleeding is expected to manage until a guard decides she deserves a sanitary napkin."

I don't think it was the Kotex that made me cry. I think my feelings about Sandra's death finally caught up to me, and the image of a woman in a bleak prison cell, her baby gone from her, her legs streaming with the blood of her loss, a wad of saturated cotton sodden between her thighs, just set me off. I lay my head down on the table and wept. I wept for Sandra and for all those other women, some of whom had made terrible decisions, others who had had miseries foisted upon them. I wept for those mothers who labored in shackles, had their babies torn from their arms, and then watched their blood flow onto the floors of their grim and lonely cells.

I felt two gentle hands smooth my hair. We sat like that for a few moments, this kind and generous woman whom I knew not at all and I; she stroking my hair while I cried. When I finally looked up, she cupped my cheek with her hand. Her touch was tender, and yet sure and strong. I could so clearly imagine her delivering a child.

"Do you remember anything about the people who took Sandra's baby?" I asked. "Anything at all?"

"They came right away—I don't think she'd been in labor for more than two hours when they arrived. One of the nurses came in and told me they were there, in the waiting room in Labor and Delivery. I had them sent to wait in Recovery so that Sandra could have a few hours with her son. I didn't see them. Her patient record will include some information. It has to indicate to whom the baby was released. It usually says the name of the foster care agency and the name of the social worker from the Department of Social Services. I remember that this case was unusual because the foster parents came on their own."

"But those records are confidential. I can't get them."

A weary, sad smile flitted across her face. "You can't, but I can."

# Fourteen

Two days later, when I had all but given up on her, Lois Curtin called me with the names of the couple with whom baby Noah Lorgeree had been placed. I ran a skip trace on them and found them easily enough, on Alcatraz Avenue in Oakland. The address was recent, and the phone number came up listed with the bill paid through the end of the month. I had them.

"Oh no," I muttered under my breath, staring at the computer screen.

"What?" Peter said.

I'd waited until after I put the kids to bed to begin work on the computer, and the house was pleasantly quiet. Quiet enough to hear the symphony of competing appliances—dishwasher, washing machine, dryer.

"I have to go back up to northern California."

The obscenity Peter used was one of those words he specifically keeps out of his screenplays in order not to run afoul of the Motion Picture Association of America's PG rating.

"What is wrong with you?" I asked.

"What's wrong with me? What do you think is wrong with me? This will be your third trip in a little over a week."

This had never happened to us before. Never had Peter been anything but supportive of my career, no matter how burgeoning, no matter how little money I made, no matter how foolhardy my job would strike anyone else. All the other feminist men my girlfriends and I went to college with, the ones who marched by our sides in Take Back the Night marches, who protested sex-segregated fraternities with us, who took Intro to Women's History as their freshman American Studies elective, those men had all ended up as versions of their fathers, working twelve-hour days and expecting to come home to immaculate homes and above-average children whose homework was done and already in their backpacks waiting to be handed in to the teachers in the morning. Peter was one of the few husbands who didn't mind a messy house, filthy children, and dinner from a bucket or paper bag. Not so long as his wife was satisfied and content. Most women I knew were complying with their husbands' expectations. A few were still working, but many had left their jobs as pediatric neurologists or partners in law firms or studio executives, and had become full-time mothers. It went without saying that the stay-at-home moms did all the child care and housework, whatever wasn't contracted out. What was stranger was that the working mothers did it, too. But Peter was different from my friends' husbands. He did more or less his fair share, and didn't object when I tried to carve out some sort of career in the few hours between car pool runs. Or at least he hadn't until now.

"I don't have a choice, Peter. The couple that fostered the baby is in Oakland."

It was just stress. That's the only explanation for why we ended up standing inches apart, our faces red, screaming at each other. Peter said things like, "You aren't around when I need you," and I said things like, "You aren't being supportive." It's even possible someone screamed, "I hate you," at the top of his or her lungs. Like I said, it was all just stress. We were exhausted, stretched to the breaking point by sleep deprivation and worries, Peter about his lawsuit, me about Sandra's murder and her lost son. We loved each other as much as we ever did, and we didn't mean any of it.

But try explaining that to a four-year-old.

Isaac stood in one of the balcony nooks overlooking the living room. He was sucking on the neck of his pajama shirt and rocking back and forth, holding on to the iron railing. His low moans were virtually inaudible from so far above our heads. I noticed him only because he was wearing a pair of Ruby's bright-orange-and-pink-striped long underwear, and the flash of brilliant color caught my eye. The pajamas were much too big for him, and the long cuffs drooped over his wrists and ankles, covering his hands and feet.

"Oh, baby," I crooned, looking up at him.

Peter followed my gaze. He swore softly under his breath. We ran up the stairs and within a few moments I was holding Isaac, who by now was crying uncontrollably, his little bird body shaking with sobs. Only his cheeks retained any baby softness now; the rest of him was all knobby, little-boy bones. Snuggling him was like cuddling a Tinkertoy.

"Sweetie," I said. "Mama and Daddy were just having a little argument. We're okay."

He burrowed his head into my belly. Peter patted ineffectually at his back.

"It's all right, buddy," he said.

Isaac moaned.

"You've seen us fight before, kiddo," I said. "Lots of times. Mama and Daddy fight, and then we make up. Just like you and Ruby. See, now we're making up. Watch." I pried his face loose from my waist and lifted him out of my lap. His eyes and nose were streaming and I wiped them with the tail of his shirt.

"I love you, Daddy," I said brightly.

"I love you, too," Peter replied, equally falsely.

"And I'm so sorry for all the mean things I said."

"Me, too."

Isaac looked from one of us to the other, part of him wanting desperately to believe that it could be over so easily, part of him disgusted with what was obviously a sham.

"See?" I said. "Mama and Daddy are all made up."

"For good?" Isaac whispered.

"Of course."

"For forever?"

"Of course."

Peter said, "That doesn't mean we're not going to fight again, bud. That happens, God knows. Especially when a person is married to someone like your mother. But I'm going to try to be more patient in the future."

I opened my mouth, all set to resume with a fresh blast of fury, but caught myself in time. Peter smiled at me and mouthed the words, "I'm sorry."

I saw him then, as I hadn't for the past few minutes. It's strange what happens when we fight. When we argue it's as though I am no longer able to recognize that standing before me is the person I love. Instead, I see only this *opponent*. Now, suddenly, when he made a joke and whispered a real apology, the red haze lifted from my eyes and I could recognize him again.

"I love you," I said. This time there was no falseness in my tone.

"Me, too."

"Me, too," Isaac interjected.

"Bedtime for you, my friend," I said as I heaved him up into my arms. "And for me, too."

"Juliet, why don't we all go with you?" Peter said as he walked us down the hall to Isaac's bedroom. "There's an animation studio up near San Francisco that's in the running for the TV series. I wouldn't mind checking out their setup. And the kids have never been to San Francisco. We can ride the cable car."

"What about school?" I said.

"So they'll miss coloring and Legos for a couple of days. It won't kill them."

I rested my cheek against the top of Isaac's head. "Okay," I said. "I'll go online and find a hotel as soon as I get him to sleep."

# Fifteen

THE next day—as I wolfed cucumber sandwiches and tried to convince the wretchedly behaved royalty with whom I was forced to experience San Francisco's finest Prince and Princess Tea to stop lobbing scones at one another's heads—I could not help but contrast this San Francisco vacation to the ones Peter and I had taken in years past. Back then we'd chosen our hotels based on criteria other than the availability of cribs and children's room service menus. We'd spent our days wandering through the Hayes and Noe valleys, shopping the hyper-funky boutiques. We'd gone to old movies at the Castro Theater and roamed the streets snapping bad photographs of adorable Victorian houses.

"Look, Mama!" Isaac interrupted my reverie. "Ruby braided my hair with her princess stick."

She had indeed managed to interlace her scepter, a foot-long, rainbow-colored lollipop, through his feathery hair.

"Ruby," I said, the threat in my low voice so frightening that a dozen juvenile princes and princesses in our immediate vicinity clung in abject terror to their mothers. "If you licked that lollipop before you put it on Isaac's head you are going to be in the worst trouble of your life."

A buzz cut, it turns out, is an oddly easy thing to track down on a Friday afternoon in downtown San Francisco. By the time we were due to meet Peter back at the hotel, Isaac's long, floppy hair had been shorn to regulation military length by a friendly Filipino barber. Isaac was the proud owner of a new San Francisco Giants baseball cap, which I hoped would help warm his newly denuded scalp.

The next morning we set out for the cable car, me carrying Sadie strapped to my front in the Baby Bjorn, newly bald Isaac wearing yet another new hat, this time a San Francisco Giants ski cap, and Ruby skipping along by my side. Peter was talking on his cell phone, as he'd been doing all morning. His "litigation team" had set up yet another conference call and Peter was hard at work in his designated role, cursing Macramé Man and bemoaning the frivolity of the lawsuit. He kept it up on the line to the cable car and all the way up Powell Street to Ghirardelli Square. He's a good father, though, so despite being involved in his telephone call, he managed to catch Isaac when the kid swung from the bar of the cable car into oncoming traffic.

I think Ruby and Isaac enjoyed themselves. I hope someone did, because I sure as hell didn't. It's hard to have fun when you're in an ice cream parlor, breastfeeding a baby, wrangling two rambunctious small children up to their ears in hot fudge and whipped cream, while dodging the dirty looks of the people at the next table who don't appreciate your husband's loud cell phone conversation, his profanity, or the dollops of chocolate chip mint that keep landing on the backs of their necks.

Is it any wonder that Peter and I ended up having a fight on the pier? Thank heavens the kids were distracted by the barking sea lions, otherwise they would have been terrified. It always amazes me how a married couple can carry on a screaming fight in whispers. The volume may be low, but the facial expressions make up for it. Peter would have said this one started when I tore the ear bud out of his ear and flung it in San Fransisco Bay. I beg to differ. In my opinion it began when his cell phone rang that morning.

We both agree on how it ended, or at least how hostilities ceased for the time being. I stormed off with Sadie and hopped in a cab, leaving Peter by himself to manage his conference call and the family outing to Alcatraz.

Forty-five minutes later, I was in Oakland in front of what my skip trace had come up with as the address for Nancy and Jason McDonnell, shaking my head in surprise at the state of the building. Most foster families aren't wealthy or even upper middle class. Those of us who are comfortably off don't usually open up our homes to the less privileged. I've always been amazed that it is quite often the very people who have the least who are the most generous. Still, this level of decrepitude seemed too much.

The building was a ramshackle three-family

house covered in peeling siding. The front porch hung crazily from one railing, the other side collapsed into a pile of splintered boards. Half the windows were broken, some taped up with duct tape, others covered in cardboard, and others simply left with jagged cracks. Still, the house was in better shape than the one next door, which had gone up in flames at some point and now squatted, a hulking, charred reminder of how little anyone cared about this part of Oakland.

I sniffed the air, wondering if my infant's lungs were being filled with bits of ashen asbestos and if I should turn and make a run for it. But I had come all this way, and had had a horrible fight with Peter. I couldn't bear to go home empty-handed.

I circled the house, hoping to find a back or side entrance as the front was obviously too treacherous to attempt even without a baby strapped to my chest. Instead, what I stumbled across was a young couple, huddled on the back steps, sharing a joint.

"Hi," I said.

"Hey," the man replied with barely a glance in my direction. His whole body was curved around the joint like a question mark. Everything about him was long and thin, as if he were a fractal-person, composed of long, thin fingers on long, thin hands, dangling at the ends of long, thin arms under a long, thin face with long, lank hair, all atop a long, thin body. I couldn't see them, but I was sure his feet and toes were long and thin, too. He was also dirty. Not filthy, but just a little bit greasy.

His friend was his twin, although they looked nothing alike. She was dark and small. But she had no more flesh covering her bones than he did, and she gave the same impression of being covered with a thin layer of grime. She had a down jacket draped over her shoulders, under which she wore only a dirty white tank top. Her arms were dappled with track marks, both fresh ones and others that had long since healed over. This case was causing me to spend an awful lot of time with junk addicts.

"I'm looking for Nancy and Jason McDonnell," I said. "Do you know how I can get to their apartment?"

The man took a long drag off his joint and looked up at me, as if he was finally really registering my presence in the yard. His gaze lingered on Sadie for a moment. Then, as if dismissing any possible threat we could pose, he shrugged. "That's us."

"You're Jason McDonnell?"

If he noticed the horror in my voice at the thought that these two bedraggled, hollow-eyed junkies were the people I was looking for, he did not show it. "Jase. Nobody calls me Jason. Now you know who I am, why don't you tell me who you are?"

"Mind if I pull up a seat? My neck is killing me from dragging this baby around." Sadie was getting too big and fat for the Baby Bjorn, but I hadn't wanted to pull her stroller onto the cable car. Another reason to be angry at Peter. If we hadn't had a fight I wouldn't have stormed off to Oakland without the stroller.

The woman pointed to a rusted metal garden chair across the packed-dirt yard. I pulled it over and sat down. Sadie had fallen asleep, and I hoped that the sudden lack of motion wouldn't wake her up. I rocked back and forth a bit to simulate walking. Not that that would fool her for an instant.

"I'm Juliet Applebaum," I said. "I'm here about your foster son."

"Which one?" Jase said.

"You have more than one?"

"We don't have any right now, because we're, like, on temporary hold pending investigation, but we've had a bunch. I don't know how many. Nancy, what is it? Six? Seven?"

"Seven," she said.

"I'm talking about Noah Lorgeree."

The woman drew back from me, and Jase's face shut down. His fingers twitched spasmodically. He took a long pull on the joint and passed it to Nancy. "We don't know nothing about that one."

I was about to start wheedling, smiling, doing a song and dance to get the information, but I suddenly realized that was going to get me exactly nowhere with these two.

"You know what?" I said, leaning forward, the cold metal of the chair pressing against the backs of my legs. "Let's not even start this, okay? You don't care, I don't have the energy for it, and my daughter's going to wake up hungry in about ten minutes."

I reached into my purse and pulled out my wallet. I quickly counted the cash. Thank God I'd gone to the ATM in preparation for this trip. "There's five hundred dollars for you right now if you tell me what happened to the baby. I don't know what you two are using besides that joint, but I'm pretty sure it's heroin. What's the street value nowadays? One hundred, one hundred fifty a gram? So even if you want to buy a handful of roofies to max out your high, you'll still get a good three or four grams with what I'm giving you. That's a nice little chunk, isn't it? More than you've got stashed in your apartment, I'll bet."

They stared at me, open-mouthed. That's usually the response I get when I exhibit a familiarity with a culture more dangerous than the soccer-mom milieu that people often assume I belong to. It's not that I look particularly straight, although I'm not tattooed and have no piercings other than those that were considered de rigueur among Jewish American Princesses growing up in New Jersey in the 1980s—earlobes, two in each because I had a wild side. But I get my hair cut at an über-funky L.A. salon because that's where Stacey insists I go, and my clothes, while certainly designed to camouflage my corpulent behind and upper arms, possess a certain ragged, urban chic. I really don't think I look like a complete suburban mom. But it doesn't really matter; strap on a Baby Bjorn or saddle up a baby stroller, and to the rest of the world—the non-mommy world—you fall into that amorphous, asexual, a-cool category. Other mothers make the distinctions—we know the subtle difference between the sling-wearing, attachment-parenting, co-sleeping moms; the top-tier-nursery-school, Bugaboo-stroller-pushing, Pilates-reformer-straddling moms; the barbed-wire-tattooed, Zutano-baby-clothes-buying, never-listens-to-Raffi, funky-hip moms; the soccer-chai-with-drink-cup, nursery-school committee, carpool-queen moms. *We* know how to distinguish one from the other, but to the rest of the world we're all just moms. And moms are certainly not supposed to know that Rohypnol enhances a heroin high.

"Five hundred?" the woman said. She looked about thirty years old. Actually, she looked about a hundred and thirty, but I could tell she was more or less thirty years old. A little younger than me.

"If you tell me where the baby is."

"And if we don't know?"

"You tell me what you do know and I'll give you three hundred. That's still three grams or so."

"Two grams. I won't use chiva, and china white's one fifty a gram."

I waited. Jase ground out the joint on the edge of the top stair and then slipped the roach into the pocket of his filthy jeans.

"Three hundred?" he said.

"Start at the beginning. How did you get involved? Who contacted you about Sandra Lorgeree's baby?" Sadie began to stir and I got to my feet. While I waited for one of them to answer, I began rocking back and forth, hoping to lull her into a few more minutes of sleep.

"We got a call," Nancy said. "Some lady called us and asked us if we wanted to earn twenty-five hundred bucks."

"That's not what happened," Jase said. "First she asked us if we were the Jason and Nancy McDonnell who were licensed foster care parents in Alameda County. And if we'd been foster parents to"—he frowned—"damn, what was that kid's name? The one who got us into all the trouble?"

"Roshaun."

"Right, Roshaun. She asked us if we'd been Roshaun's foster parents. The little brat got busted stealing DVDs from Blockbuster. She asked us if we had been his foster parents, and I was like, 'Yeah, so what? You can't pin that on us, man. We're being investigated because of that little sucker, but it's not our fault. That kid was messed up before he got here.' But she said she didn't care about Roshaun. She just wanted to make sure we still had our licenses. That they hadn't been taken away yet. I said no, they haven't taken our licenses, but social services is still investigating that Roshaun case, and they said they aren't going to place any kids here until they're done. *Then* she asked us if we wanted to earn twenty-five hundred bucks."

I continued rocking back and forth and Sadie settled back down. The McDonnells seemed to find my motion soothing, too. It was either the rocking or the thought of the two grams of heroin they were going to be shooting into their veins over the next day or so. The looked almost hypnotized. "Who was she? Did you find out her name?" I said.

"No," Nancy said. "We never even saw her. She told us we'd get a packet in the mail with the forms to fill out, and that we'd get a call on the day the baby was born. She even sent a cell phone for us to keep with us. Can you believe that?"

Jase laughed. "It was like, perfect timing, too, because Nancy's cell phone service was cut off a few months before."

Nancy said, "The driver took the phone back, though, when he took the baby."

My heart sank. "The driver? What driver?"

She shivered and pulled her down coat more tightly around her shoulders. It wasn't particularly cold, but she had so little flesh insulating her bones. "A driver came to pick us up when the prisoner . . . what was her name?"

"Sandra Lorgeree."

"Right, Sandra. When Sandra went into labor, the woman called us just like she said she would. She sent a car and driver to take us up to the hospital by Dartmore. The driver had everything in the car. Everything the baby would need. You know, a car seat and diapers. Formula and bottles. Even a little outfit. The driver waited in the car in the parking lot the whole time we were inside. Then, when they released the baby to us, he drove us down here and dropped us off."

"And the baby?"

Nancy shrugged.

"You just left the baby in the car?"

"Look," Jase said. "That was the agreement. We were just supposed to pick the baby up, not keep him. Anyway, we don't do newborns."

Even in their addled state they must have sensed something in my expression, some surprise, some disgust. How could a system, even one as under-funded and overwhelmed as the foster care system, entrust two such obvious miscreants with the lives of children?

"We've been fostering kids a long time," Nancy said defensively.

"Yeah," Jase said. "We can clean up pretty good when we need to."

"How did you start, if you don't mind my asking?" Not that I cared if they minded.

Jase leaned back on the step. "My parents did it. They always had a couple of foster kids running around the house. It's not bad money, you know? Especially if you take a special-needs kid. That's what we usually do, right Nancy? You get a bonus for the special-needs kids."

I looked at Nancy, who had begun dotting her finger along one of the healing track marks on her arm, as if in preparation for spending my money. She didn't reply to his question.

"Can you remember what kind of car took you to the prison?" I asked.

"I dunno," Jase said. "Fancy. Black. Right, Nancy? Like a Cadillac or something."

"Maybe a Mercedes," Nancy said.

"So it was either a Cadillac or a Mercedes?" I said.

"Yeah," Jase said. "Something like that."

"But it was definitely black?"

"Or maybe blue. Not white. Definitely not white."

"Do you remember anything else? The license plate number?"

"No."

"Anything about the driver? Was he wearing a uniform? Did he have an accent? Was he white, black?"

"He was a white guy," Jase said.

"No he wasn't," Nancy said. "He was Filipino. Or Mexican. I think."

Oh, the joys of eyewitness identification. I wasn't going to get anything useful out of these two. The best they could give me was either a blue or black car, and the driver was probably not African American. Although, given the state of their inebriation, he was probably a Maasai tribesman driving a fuchsia Humvee.

I took the wad of cash and handed it to Jase along with one of my business cards. "Call me if you think of anything else," I said.

Jase licked his thumb and began counting his money. Nancy hung over his shoulder, smiling avariciously at the stack of bills. Neither noticed when Sadie and I walked out of their miserable yard and away from their horrible lives.

Sadie and I met our family back at the hotel. It was the second time Peter and I had had to make up in as many days, and we were both feeling pretty sheepish. My experience with the loathsome McDonnells had made me appreciate him all the more, and I gathered he had come to feel something similar while trapped on a rocky prison island with no cellular service and only our children for company. The nadir of his day had been when Isaac got lost, causing the National Park Service to come to a crashing halt while every ranger and tourist on the island ran up and down the island's craggy paths and rusted stairwells screaming Isaac's name. Peter had panicked, convinced Isaac had flung himself into the sea in an attempted reenactment of Clint Eastwood's daring escape. It turned out that he had merely locked himself into a porta-potty.

Whatever the reason for our rapprochement, Peter and I were very happy to see each other, and had we not been trapped in a single hotel room with three small children, we might even have been inspired to celebrate the end of our quarrel in a fitting manner. As it was, we were limited to room service and in-room movies.

When the children were finally asleep, I recounted the horror of my day. "Whoever set this up, whoever took Noah, must have had some connection to the foster care system. I'm assuming it was a woman because it was a woman who contacted Sandra and it was a woman who hired Jase and Nancy. She knew that the baby would only be released to a licensed foster care provider, and she had access to information that allowed her to find a couple who still had a license but were sufficiently dishonest and corrupt that they would do whatever she asked."

"Who could it be?" Peter said. He was leaning up against the headboard of the queen bed we were sharing with Sadie. Ruby and Isaac were curled up together like puppies in the other bed. They got along so well when they were asleep.

"I haven't the faintest idea. In fact, I'm all out of ideas. This is driving me insane. Now I know for sure that someone stole that baby, but I can't even begin to figure out who, or why. I can tell you one thing, though. I just know that Sandra's murder wasn't an act of random prison gang violence. It's connected to this. It has to be."

"What will you do if you do find the baby?" Peter asked.

I moved Sadie from one breast to the other. "I don't honestly know. I better start looking for Sandra's family. I should probably figure out whether they even want the baby before I do anything else. If they don't, then what? Even if I succeed, I'll have tracked Noah down only to deliver him right back to the foster care system."

# sixteen

THE next day, when we returned to Los Angeles, I called Al and found him finally busy on a case referred by Harold Brodsky. Despite the fact that we'd just flown in that morning, I decided to take the kids to school, and now I was driving down the freeway, debating whether to go to the office or "work" from home. I had a mountain of laundry that was calling my name, which would normally be a good reason to head down to Westminster.

"I guess I could try to find Sandra's aunt and cousins," I said.

"Already on it," Al said.

"What do you mean, you're already on it? You're

on Brodsky's case." Al was supposed to be figuring out how to keep a brawling young actor from being sued by someone who had beat *him* up in a bar fight.

"Not me. Chiki."

"How is Chiki tracking people if he's not allowed to work on the computer and not allowed to travel?" I swerved to avoid a large SUV that was drifting perilously close to my lane. The driver was talking on her cell phone and applying lipstick. I'd never try to do *both* at once while driving. One or the other, but not both. "You know what?" I said. "Don't tell me. I don't care. Let this be your and Chiki's problem. I'm going to go talk to some more junkies. I can't seem to get enough of junkies nowadays. Let me know if some paying work comes in that I should be doing instead."

Twenty minutes later, as I strapped Sadie's car seat into its wheels in preparation for our perambulation through Eagle Rock, Sandra's old neighborhood, I tried to reassure myself that, contrary to popular belief, exposure to microbes is actually good for babies. How, I reasoned, could an immune system develop in a perfectly sterile environment? Moreover, my own mattress was probably far more

bug-ridden than anything we would come across today or anything Sadie had been exposed to at the
McDonnells'. I made another mental note to find
out where one orders a handmade mattress in an
odd size.

Eagle Rock is a small neighborhood nestled between downtown L.A. and Pasadena. Considering
that it's home to Occidental College, it has a surprising number of beat-up houses, more than its
share of pit bulls barking behind chain-link fences,
and the world's ugliest and most degenerate shopping mall, Eagle Rock Plaza. However, it also has a
bunch of urban-chic coffee shops, a strong sense of
community, and "Snapshot Day," when the neighbors all take pictures of one another for their family
albums. It's one of those neighborhoods that seems
to be perennially on the verge of "gentrification,"
with all the community outrage that that tends to inspire. It's named for an actual rock, a huge monster
of a thing on the top of which hot springs have supposedly etched an eagle in flight. Personally I think
it looks more like Yosemite Sam's mustache.

I pushed the stroller down Colorado Boulevard,
which I figured was grim enough to be a hangout for
the kind of person I was hoping to find. I was look-

ing for a specific type of dealer or user, not one of the young black or brown men the cops like to bust. I was looking for white kids, kids like Nancy and Jase might have been ten years ago. I was looking for white kids with dreadlocks, pierced tongues, elaborate tattoos that implied an adolescence with at least some money to spare for body art.

The first five or six people I spoke to either didn't know Sandra's boyfriend or weren't talking. But then I found two perfect specimens out in front of a bar. They were crouched on the sidewalk, playing with a small white rat, a paper cup of change set before them in case any passersby felt inspired to make a donation.

"Hi," I said. "Cute rat." Let me be clear. There is no such thing as a cute rat. All rodents are hideous and vile and were the world to be rid of them in a single fell swoop of extermination, I would be thrilled, the food chain be damned. Still. Interrogation is an art form.

"Isn't she though?" one of the girls said. "Her name is Squeaky. But not because she's a rat or anything." She picked up the rat and kissed it. I struggled not to gag. "We named her after Squeaky Fromm."

"That's even better. So, ladies," I said. I reached into my front pocket and pulled out a five-dollar bill. I held it in my hand. "Where's Tweezer today?"

"Tweezer?" the rat-kisser said.

I sighed, folded up the bill, and made as if to shove it back in my pocket.

"We know him!" the other girl said. "We just haven't seen him for a couple of weeks."

"Shut up!" the rat-kisser hissed.

"Why?" the other girl said. "What difference does it make? Anyway, I want a mocha latte and we've got, like, no money."

"When's the last time you saw him?" I asked.

"I dunno, like a month ago, maybe? A little more. He used to live here, in an apartment up on Casper. But then his old lady got busted and he moved out. He still hung out, though. We'd see him around, doing this and that."

"But you haven't seen him in a month?"

She frowned. "Maybe a little more. I don't know. Hey, can you make that ten bucks instead of five?"

"If you give me the name of someone who might know more than you do."

The girl with the rat said, "You can try Kate.

She's a friend of his girlfriend's. If anyone knows, she will. I want ten dollars, too."

"Do you know Kate's last name?"

"Yeah, I do. My sister went to high school with her. It's Gage."

"Where can I find this Kate Gage?"

"She works at Swork, that coffee shop down the street. Hey, baby, you wanna see Squeaky?" She held her rodent toward Sadie, who batted her hands at the wriggling monstrosity. I spun the stroller around, whipped a twenty out of my wallet, and handed it to the other girl. "Thanks," I said, tearing down the block before they could infect my baby with bubonic plague.

Swork was all blond wood, stainless-steel industrial ceilings and tables, and funk. It was packed with the usual L.A. hipster screenwriting wannabes, tap-tapping on their laptops and Web-surfing on the wireless network. Ben Harper was playing on the sound system and the coffee I ordered was called Mellow-D. As I sipped my coffee and nursed Sadie, I thought to myself that this was yet another thing that Ruby would not have been victim to. When breastfeeding my first child, I not only avoided broccoli, onions, alcohol, secondhand smoke, and rodent-wielding panhandlers, but I even did my best to steer clear of caffeine. Here I was simultaneously lactating and ingesting coffee. If I wasn't careful, I was going to end up on La Leche League's Top Ten Most Wanted list.

After Sadie and I had both had our fill, I approached the young woman behind the counter.

"Kate?" I asked.

She pointed across the café to another woman, this one a little older. She was busing tables, wiping them down with a blue cloth. Carrying Sadie over my shoulder, I crossed the room.

"Hi, Kate," I said. "I knew your friend Sandra. I'm so sorry for your loss."

She stood up and put a hand out to steady herself. "Do I know you?" she asked. Her dyed black hair accentuated her yellow-tinged skin, and there was something disturbing about the way she looked, with her severely short bangs and the ragged locks hanging around her jaw. The 1940s tight-waisted housedress and thick-soled shoes she wore didn't do anything to alleviate this impression.

"I knew Sandra," I repeated. "Do you have a minute? Can we talk?"

She hesitated, and then sat down. She hovered over her chair as though unsure whether she really wanted to be there, as if she might get up and run at any moment. I explained who I was, and how it was that I'd come to know her friend. I told her about my suspicions regarding Sandra's death. I watched her face lose its wary expression.

"I'm trying to find Tweezer," I said, finally.

She frowned. "There's no way he would know anything. Even if Sandra told him something, he's likely to have forgotten it by now. Without Sandra around, Tweezer's totally lost. He's like a little kid."

I settled Sadie across my lap and rocked her gently. "I honestly don't know who else to talk to, Kate."

"But if you really think that Sandra's murder had something to do with all this, with her baby being taken, then it's crazy to think Tweezer had anything to do with it. He'd never hurt Sandra, he loved her. She was like his mother. She did everything for him. The whole idea is nuts anyway; the guy can't arrange a trip to the grocery store, let alone a contract killing." Putting Sandra's death into such brutal words clearly caused her pain, and Kate's mouth trembled. For a moment, she looked like she was going to cry.

"Do you know Tweezer's real name?"

"Yeah, didn't Sandra tell you? He's Gabriel Francisco Arguello."

I'm sure my jaw dropped. The Arguello family is as close as California gets to landed gentry. They make even the Gettys look like nouveau-riche carpetbaggers. The Arguellos received their land grants from the kings of Spain and, despite a minor reversal of fortune during the Mexican-American War in 1848, they managed to retain a significant portion of their northern California holdings, including a few acres not too far from Coloma. Between the gold they later found on that land and their prime San Francisco real estate, the family had been pretty well set up ever since.

"Are you telling me that Tweezer's father was Frank Arguello, the mayor of San Francisco?" I said.

"No, that was his grandfather. Tweezer's dad died when he was just a kid. His mom was in politics, though. I think it's pretty much the family business. She used to be on the San Francisco Board of Supervisors and I think his uncle is the lieutenant governor or something."

"I know," I said. "I voted for him."

"Do you want more coffee?" Kate said suddenly.

I shook my head. She rose unsteadily and poured herself a cup. Then she sat down and took a tentative sip.

"For the longest time my doctor told me I wasn't supposed to have any coffee, which was fine, because it made me feel really sick. But now he says it might actually be good for my liver. So I'm allowed to have it again."

My confusion must have been evident.

"I have hepatitis C," Kate explained. "That's the bad kind. And I have an exceptional case. People can usually live for decades with this disease, but mine is proceeding really quickly. I'm finally a prodigy at something, and it's hep C. That's probably why Sandra never asked me to take Noah for her. I have a hard enough time taking care of myself, let alone a baby. And, well, I guess she wasn't sure I'd be around for him. I might not be. Not without a liver transplant."

"I'm so sorry," I said.

She shrugged. "Yeah, it sucks. The crazy thing is, I was always real careful, you know? I didn't want to get AIDS, so I snorted my heroin. That way

I never had to share needles. I didn't know you could pass hep C through the straws. It just never occurred to me."

"I'm so sorry," I repeated. It seemed like the only thing to say.

"I felt bad for Sandra. Here she was having this baby, and her best friend was too sick to take him, and the baby's father was too strung out to do anything. She had nowhere to turn."

"What about Gabriel's parents? Why didn't she go to them?"

Kate immediately shook her head. "She would never. *Never.* Gabriel's mom is a complete witch. She destroyed his life. Why do you think the poor kid turned out the way he did? And Gabriel's stepfather, well, Sandra had issues with him. She would never have considered giving Noah to them. They would be her *last* choice. The very last place she'd turn."

Kate did not know where Tweezer was; she hadn't seen him in nearly a month, since long before Sandra was killed. She had little information for me at all, in fact. She missed her friend, she was ill, and she was barely holding it together. Finally, when I realized that our conversation was going nowhere, I took a business card out of the pack I kept in Sadie's diaper bag.

"Please call me if you hear from him," I said.

"Okay," she said, shrugging. "But I won't. Tweezer and I weren't close or anything. Sandra was my friend. And without her, there really isn't any reason for Tweezer and me to see each other, you know?"

# Seventeen

I was getting heartily sick of commuter air travel. I couldn't believe there were people who actually did this on a daily basis. Sadie, for her part, was getting to be a perfect little flyer, not even uttering a peep when we took off and landed, nursing right through the change in cabin pressure.

I timed my arrival at the palatial Arguello family home in the Pacific Heights neighborhood of San Francisco for 9:30 in the morning, early enough to catch them at home on a Saturday, I hoped, but not so early as to be rude. The graceful Renaissance Revival house was perched on the top of a hill overlooking the bay, and the long loggias along two sides of the house made good use of the view. The house was pale gold brick, not a common building material in a city of earthquakes, with marble arches around the doors and windows.

Determined not to be any more overburdened in this interview than was absolutely necessary, and not eager to schlep more than I had to up the imposing front steps, I left my car seat and wheels on the sidewalk.

With Sadie buckled into her Baby Bjorn and staring around her with wide, unblinking eyes, and an extra diaper and the packet of wipes tucked into my purse, I made my way up the steps and rang the bell. After a few minutes, an ancient crone heaved open the door. She wore a stiff black uniform complete with a white ruffled headpiece, just like something out of a British costume drama. The massive oak door was clearly much too heavy for her, but when I moved forward to help she nearly bit my head off.

"I've got it!"

I halted with my hand halfway extended, feeling like a reprimanded schoolgirl. When the door was completely open, the elderly housemaid said, "Did you see the sign?" My eyes followed her gnarled, pointed finger. The discreet, brass-framed sign read, in impeccable calligraphy on the finest of card-stock, NO SOLICITING.

"I'm not soliciting," I said. "I'm here to see Mrs. Arguello."

The old woman sniffed doubtfully. "Is she expecting you?"

"No, but she'll want to see me. It's about her grandson."

She gasped and covered her mouth with her hand. "Is that . . ." she pointed at Sadie. "Is that . . ."

"No, no. This is *my* baby. My daughter."

She sagged against the door, relieved. I was beginning to worry that my visit was going to give the poor woman a heart attack. She looked at least eighty years old, and I couldn't believe they still forced her to work. You'd think they would have pensioned her off long ago.

"Please wait in the foyer," she said.

I cooled my heels on black marble. I'll say this about detective work, it has the unusual effect of bringing a person into contact with both the very downtrodden and the very rich. In my experience, those firmly placed in the middle class were rarely my clients or the objects of my investigations. This was not the first fabulous house I'd been in since taking up investigation for a living, although it might well have been the nicest. I wracked my brain, but I could not remember ever before waiting in an entryway with what looked suspiciously like an original Turner watercolor hanging where a regular person might put a rack for car keys.

I was peering at the painting, trying to remember from my long-ago Introduction to Art History days what, exactly, a gouache was, when I heard a frightening rumble coming from the direction of my normally quiet child. I looked down and saw Sadie's face screwed into a beet-red fist.

"Oh no. Not here. Please Sadie. Not here."

But of course, with the perfect timing peculiar to all the Applebaum-Wyeth children, and probably having noticed that I left the diaper bag with its changing pad and extra outfit stuffed in the basket of the stroller parked at the bottom of the steps, Sadie had chosen that moment to befoul her diaper. I sniffed, hoping that, sound effects notwithstanding, what was going on in the Baby Bjorn could wait half an hour or so before being attended to. No such luck. Moreover, if I didn't get to it soon, there was no guarantee that we *both* weren't going to need a change of clothes. I glanced quickly around and then unbuckled Sadie and, right there on the marble floor, using every single one of the wipes I had on me, I changed one of the most disgusting diapers ever created by a human child. By the time the little old maid made her shuffling way back to the foyer, we were all ship-shape and reassembled, and I was holding in my outstretched hand something that should probably have been handed over to a toxic waste disposal service.

"Is there somewhere I can throw this away?" I asked.

"That?" she asked, horrified.

"Yes. Do you have a garbage can? And perhaps a plastic bag?"

She shuddered and wobbled away, returning a few minutes later wearing pink rubber gloves and carrying two Ziploc bags and a white kitchen trash bin liner. She held open one Ziploc bag with trembling, gloved hands. I dropped the foul-smelling diaper inside and took the bag from her and closed it. In silence we continued our elaborate disposal ritual, with her holding out each successive bag and me dropping in the terrifying and noxious item.

When the last bag was finally sealed, I rolled the whole mess into a neat bundle.

She held out her gloved hands.

"That's okay," I said, shoving the bundle into my capacious handbag. "I'm a good camper."

"Excuse me, madame?"

"Carry in, carry out."

"Excuse me, madame?"

"It's fine. I'm all set."

"One moment please." She walked creakily out of the room. After a few moments she was back, ungloved. "Right this way," she said.

I followed her through the foyer, down a corridor, and into what seemed to be a music room. There was not one but two grand pianos, one at either end of the long room. In the middle of the room, a pink striped silk sofa and a few chairs clustered around a marble fireplace. A black-haired man with a silver goatee sat in one of the armchairs, his feet up on an ottoman, reading the *Wall Street Journal*. There was something old-fashioned about the way he looked; his figure matched the Victorian lines and furnishings of the room. His clothes were not at all outlandish or old-fashioned—simple black trousers and a fawn-colored cashmere sweater, its sleeves pushed casually up his forearms. It was something about his face, his beard perhaps, that made him seem vaguely out of his time.

The woman perched on the striped sofa was more or less the same age as the man, somewhere between fifty and sixty, impeccably dressed and made up even early on a Saturday morning. Her silvery-blonde hair was coiffed in that chin-length bob that is the default hairdo for women of a certain age and class. I was distracted by it for a moment, wondering if she and her social cohorts got up every morning and teased their hair into submission, or if it was just sprayed so thoroughly that it stayed that way despite a night's sleep. Normally, at 9:30 on a Saturday morning I walk around the house looking like I'm wearing a fright wig. My only comfort is that Ruby and Peter invariably look worse.

The woman stared at me, and for a moment I could not figure out the reason for her shock. Then I realized that Sadie was the source of all the consternation. They really did not like babies in this house. Hadn't her maid warned her?

"My name is Juliet Applebaum," I said. "I'm a

private investigator. I apologize for the intrusion, and I'm sorry about this." I motioned in Sadie's general direction. "I'm afraid that nowadays for me every day is Take Your Daughter to Work Day." I was not surprised that they did not join in my forced laugh.

"Ernestine says you claim to have some information about my grandson," the woman said. "I would have refused to see you, because you see, I have no grandchildren."

She *would* have refused to see me?

"But I wonder," she said. "Have you some information about my son?"

"May I?" I hovered tentatively over a chair.

She seemed momentarily nonplussed at her own failure to offer me a seat. "Yes, yes of course, do sit down. Do you have some kind of identification?"

I pulled out my wallet and showed her my bright and shiny new private investigator's license. It's amazing how long it takes to clock enough hours to earn one of those when you're only working part-time.

"Mrs. Arguello, Mr. Arguello," I began.

"Loft."

"Excuse me?"

"My husband's name is Spencer Loft."

"Of course. I'm so sorry. Mr. Loft. Mrs. Loft,"

"Arguello."

"Excuse me?"

"I go by Arguello."

"Right, Ms. Arguello."

"Mrs."

"Mrs. Yes, well, ma'am, I was retained by Sandra Lorgeree. She was your son Gabriel's girlfriend."

She held up a well-manicured hand. "I wish to hear nothing about this girlfriend of Gabriel's. As I told my son when he called after she was arrested, I will not condone criminal conduct, nor will I condone drug use. He is not welcome in my home unless he can document his sobriety. And I will not tolerate any continued contact with that woman, even through the mail."

Sadie whimpered—the appropriate reaction, I thought—to both the tone and harshness of Gabriel's mother's words. Still, Sadie's was not a reaction necessarily useful to an interrogation. I bounced gently in my seat, hoping to shush her.

I said, "Sandra is dead, Mrs. Arguello. She was murdered in prison."

I watched her reaction very closely. It is, of course, possible to feign surprise. Actors do it all the time. For those of us who are not gifted with theatrical talent, however, shock is a difficult emotion to falsify. Suzette Arguello's jaw worked spasmodically and she leaned slightly back into the seat cushion, her hand fluttering up to her throat. Her surprise looked real.

"Murdered?" she said.

"Yes."

I turned my attention to her husband. He was sitting very still, his newspaper raised, but one corner bent. He peered over it, his brows knotted with dismay. "Good lord," he said. "How? By whom?"

"I understand that the crime is still under investigation. She was a prisoner at CCI Dartmore and was killed by another inmate."

"How tragic," Gabriel's mother murmured.

"Before Sandra was killed, she gave birth to a son, your grandson. This child was taken from her through an elaborate ruse involving the bribing of foster parents."

Again I watched her reaction. This time, I couldn't be sure, but I thought I detected a glim-

mer of something dishonest in her moue of surprise, a falseness in her exclamation of "How
shocking!"

"Do you know anything about your grandson's
whereabouts?" I asked.

"What a ridiculous question!" Spencer Loft said.
He folded his newspaper with a snap.

Mrs. Arguello stood up. "I don't see any need for
this conversation to continue, Mrs. Appleman."

"Applebaum."

"Mrs. Applebaum. My husband and I have given
you quite enough of our time."

"Do you have a current address for your son?" It
was a long shot, but I didn't have anything to lose.

"As I said before, we have not spoken to my son,
not since he called asking for money for that girl's
defense. I told him then that we would not be part of
this kind of thing, and I'm even more certain of that
now. Good day, Mrs. Applebaum. Ernestine will see
you out."

She glared at me until I rose and turned to the
door, where the elderly maid awaited my departure.
Ernestine saw me down the hall and wordlessly
hauled open the massive front door.

At the bottom of the front steps, I settled Sadie

into her car seat on wheels. Then I took the diaper out of my purse and looked around for a garbage pail. Halfway up the block I saw three large plastic bins on wheels—a blue, a black, and a green. I made my way up the steep hill. The bins were labeled for different kinds of waste. I usually leave the Dumpster-diving part of our job to Al, who doesn't really mind it. He was a cop; he's used to scraping the bottom of disgusting barrels. Despite my familiarity with what comes out of either end of a baby, I'm not particularly eager to rifle through people's trash. But my partner was four hundred miles away, and there was something in the black bin that caught my eye. In a knotted white plastic garbage bag, I was sure I saw the telltale pale blue caterpillar lumps of a string of Diaper Genie refuse. There was no way around it. I was going to have to check. I reached into the garbage bin and tore open the bag. I was right. In the bag was the long string of plastic-wrapped diapers collected by a Diaper Genie.

I checked to see if the bins were marked to indicate what address they belonged to. Alas, they were not. More frustratingly, they were situated more or less equally between the Arguello family mansion and their neighbor's somewhat less ostentatious abode. Either the bins belonged to their neighbors, or there was a baby in the Arguello house.

Sadie began her pre-wailing murmuring and I dropped the lid of the bin. The next half hour was spent in a progressively more frantic search for a café in which to wash my hands and nurse the baby. By the time we had accomplished that and I had hauled Sadie back up the unbelievably steep hill to the Arguello house, it was clear to me that the family was gone. Heavy curtains had been drawn across the loggias, giving the house a shuttered and shut-down look.

I wandered around the periphery of the mansion for a few minutes, hoping to catch a glimpse of something—a mobile hanging in a window, a stroller handle peeping from the garage—but no such luck. Finally, I called a cab and took myself and Sadie back to the airport, somewhat the wiser for my excursion, but no less confused.

# Eighteen

WHEN the cab finally pulled into our narrow winding street in the Hollywood Hills, after being stuck in a mysterious Saturday afternoon traffic jam on the 101, we found ourselves trapped behind a truck that had worked itself halfway into a ditch. Despite the fact that the truck was clearly jammed tight and going nowhere, its driver had decided to unload from the trailer the largest mattress I had ever seen in my life. It took four men to lift the thing, one of them my elated husband. He had managed to work his way under the mattress, deciding for some reason that he could best assist the movers by balancing the thing on his back. He was calling useless directions at the three laborers, all of whom were assiduously ignoring him.

"And, heave it to the right!" Peter shouted. "Up and over."

"Honey?" I said, bending down so that I could see him.

"Surprise!" he said.

"No kidding."

"I ordered a mattress for our bed."

"I see. When?"

"Six weeks ago. Aren't you surprised?"

"Totally."

"Aren't you happy?"

"You bet. How are you guys going to get it up the stairs?"

"I have absolutely no idea."

When I greeted the movers in my semi-fluent Spanish, the foreman asked me, very politely, if I would consider asking my well-intentioned husband to allow them to do their job unassisted. I assured them that as soon as they hauled the mattress off of him, I would pin him to the ground and prevent him from aiding them any further, and that is more or less what I did. The three men managed, I have no idea how, to wrestle the monstrosity up the stairs and remove its bug- and mold-filled predecessor. By the time I had made the bed with the extra long flat sheets (fitted sheets were a pipe dream, I'm afraid) and piles of pillows and comforters from our old bed, Peter had put the baby down for a nap and settled Ruby and Isaac in front of *The Lion King 1½*.

"We have eighty-eight minutes," he said as he bounced into the bedroom. "Come here, wife."

I love him. I really do. I wish I had been in the mood. But I wasn't. "Peter, I just got off a plane. I woke up at the crack of dawn, and I've been sifting through garbage cans all day. I'm exhausted and I want to take a shower." I felt awful the moment I said it, even before I saw his face collapse and his mood turn from delighted expectation to crushed disappointment and then anger.

"Wait," I said, but he was already out the door. "Peter, wait. I'm sorry." I ran after him. "I'm sorry. I'm sorry." I stood in the hall trying to drag him back into the bedroom. "Let's break in the new bed. Come on!"

"Never mind," he said. "I'm not in the mood."

"Oh, don't be such a prima donna!" I said. "I said I'm sorry."

"*I'm* a prima donna? *I* am?" He jerked his arm out of my hands and stomped away down the hall. I stood there, listening to his footsteps as he walked down the stairs to the first floor, and then all the way to his office in the dungeon.

By Monday morning things were back to normal. We were no longer arguing, although we hadn't talked about what happened, and we hadn't done anything to welcome the new mattress into the family, unless Sadie spitting up what appeared to be at least eight ounces of breast milk on it counts. We set off for Isaac's Parent Appreciation Breakfast a fairly content—or at least not visibly discontented—family unit.

The "Bet," or B class, had gone all out decorating their room in honor of the visiting parents. The walls were hung with painted self-portraits, and I had to remind myself sternly not to compare Isaac's to those of his classmates. It wasn't my kid's fault that his hand-eye coordination skills weren't on a par with those of some of his classmates. Who would even want a child like that Rebecca Fineman, I told myself as I stared wistfully at the little girl's beautifully rendered drawing. It was an almost perfect likeness, down to the little bump on her nose and the amblyopia. Isaac had drawn one of his usual bubble-people and for some reason had given himself blue skin.

Sue and Bracha, the preternaturally even-tempered preschool teachers, called the milling parents to order, just in the nick of time, before we began tearing each other's throats out in an excess of competitive zeal. I was not the only parent unable to prevent herself from comparing her child to the others. Quite frankly, I think I was one of the only ones who bothered even to feel lousy about engaging in the fierce Olympiad of Parental Expectation. Which was a lucky thing, since my son was about to make me feel like I deserved to be given a spot in the Maternal Hall of Fame right between Jeffrey Dahmer's mother and Joseph Stalin's.

The other parents, conversely, felt just grand when the centerpiece of the Parent Appreciation Breakfast began. After we ate our booger scones and drank our tepid coffee, the children stepped to the head of the room, one at a time. Each one recited a poem written especially for his or her parents. The poems weren't long; the children were only four years old or even, like Isaac, hadn't quite reached that birthday. Each poem began, "I love my parents because . . ." and then listed three special things that the child's parents did. It was a veritable waterworks in the Bet class, as you can imagine. Every mother burst into tears as her child's piping voice recounted her delicious chocolate chip cookies or the way she kissed his boo-boos. The fathers grew too misty-eyed to work the digital camcorders when their sons talked about playing catch and reading good-night stories.

And then it was Isaac's turn. Peter and I squeezed each other's hands in delighted anticipation. Isaac stood up, sighed deeply, and then, prodded gently by Bracha, began to recite, "I love my parents because they play with me. My mom plays gin with me. It's fun because I win. My dad plays poker with me and takes my money. I love my mom because she makes really good fried chicken. I love to eat the crispy skin."

Peter and I sat holding hands, our smiles frozen on our faces. One of the mothers leaned over to me and whispered, "I must get your fried chicken recipe."

I said, "I've never made fried chicken in my life."

After the last child recited her poem, the last mother wept with joy, and the last father chuckled with pride, Peter and I sent Isaac out to play on the tricycles and cornered Bracha and Sue.

"So, here's the thing," I said. "None of that was true."

"Pardon?" Bracha said, in her thick Israeli accent.

"Isaac's poem. Nothing in it was true. I've never made fried chicken. I don't play gin with him, and Peter does not play poker with him. Peter does all the cooking in our house, and we play lots of other games. Uno, for example. And Legos." I was so worried that the teachers would be convinced that Isaac had invented the things in his poem because there was nothing at home he could come up with, no games we played or food we made. And that just wasn't true! We played with the kid all the time.

"No," Bracha said. "That's not possible. I went over the poems with each child, individually. We talked all about it. Isaac told me all about your games of cards. And the poker. He said you give

him allowance but you take it away when he loses."
She clearly didn't approve of that.

"Okay, that's just nonsense," Peter said. "Did you really believe that?"

This was definitely the wrong tack to take. "We're just sort of wondering what you recommend we do under these circumstances," I said. "We're sort of knocked for a loop here."

The two teachers exchanged glances. Bracha said, "This has never happened before, and we've been doing these poems for six years."

"He's an original, my kid," Peter said.

Did I detect a note of *pride*? I resisted the urge to kick my husband in the shins.

"Do you think this is a cry for help or something? Should we take him to a therapist?" I asked.

Bracha gave me a pitying, sorrowful smile, the kind of smile you give an insane street person who shouts a greeting as you walk past. "Perhaps you might just talk to him about it, and see why he lied. And we'll do the same."

"Right," I said. "Of course. Talk to him. That's exactly what we'll do."

We did, of course, that very evening after supper. Not that it was a particularly satisfying conversation. Isaac offered no explanation for why he had lied in his poem. Neither did he seem to care that his parents felt decidedly unappreciated.

"Do you want to write a new poem, Isaac?" I said.

"Why?"

"You could write a poem about stuff we really do with you."

Isaac shrugged.

"Or you could write a poem about why you're mad at Mama and Daddy."

Isaac gave me the look of disgust my attempt at child psychology deserved.

"Maybe it's Sadie's fault," he said.

"Sadie's fault?" I said. "How could this be Sadie's fault? Sadie's just a little baby. She wasn't even there when you wrote the poem, and she was sleeping in her car seat during the whole breakfast."

"I think it is Sadie's fault," he repeated, nodding.

"Why?"

"Because Sadie makes you tired, and then you and Daddy have fights. You should send Sadie back to the hospital. Maybe just at night, so you can sleep. Can I go play with my Bionicles and watch TV with Ruby now?"

I nodded and he skipped lightly out of the

kitchen where we had been having our little meeting. I glanced at my husband.

"Out of the mouths of babes," he said.

"Wow."

He went to the fridge and pulled out a beer. "Want half?"

"Actually, yes."

He split the beer between two glasses and handed one to me. We drank in silence for a few minutes.

I turned to Peter. "What do you think we should do?"

Peter looked at me, sadly. "Hell if I know," he said. "I've got to go to work." And with that he went down the stairs to his dungeon, closing the door behind him.

# Nineteen

"I found Sandra's aunt and cousins," Chiki said. His face did not reflect any pleasure at his success. On the contrary. He looked about as glum as I'd ever seen him.

"Give me a second to put the baby down," I said. I had Sadie draped over one arm, her arms and legs dangling like a rag doll's. It was her new favorite position.

Chiki reached out his hands, and after a moment's consideration, I handed her to him. He tucked the baby up under his chin and nuzzled her soft head. She gave him a placid and cross-eyed glance of contentment and shoved her fist in her mouth.

"She likes you," I said as I tossed my diaper bag, my purse, and the old tote into which I'd crammed my notes on the case under my desk. "So where does Sandra's aunt live? Did you talk to her?"

Chiki shook his head. "Not to her, to her daughter-in-law. Her son Jonathan's wife, Allison. They live in Reno."

"That's great," I said. "Reno's not too far away. What did you find out? What's with the long face?"

Chiki had found Bettina Trudeau easily enough. A mortgage default and a couple of bankruptcies make a person easy to track. Once you enter the system with that kind of a bang, the only way out is the witness protection program. And even then, I'll bet your creditors would find you. Wells Fargo and American Express do not give up so easily. Sandra's aunt's financial woes had washed her up on the shores of her son's largesse, and it was to his wife that Chiki spoke. It was immediately clear to Chiki that Allison Trudeau had long since come to the end of whatever patience she might once have had with the trials and tribulations of her husband's family. She had greeted the news of Sandra's incarceration, her murder, and the missing baby with a bitter laugh. She had then launched into a twenty-minute diatribe.

Was Chiki aware that Allison's mother-in-law suffered from congestive heart failure complicated by emphysema?

Was he aware that despite this diagnosis, and despite a prognosis that promised her no more than a few more months to live, Bettina persisted in smoking through the tracheotomy hole carved into the center of her throat, befouling the air Allison's children breathed and the upholstery of her furniture?

Was he aware that Bettina had begun using adult diapers, not because she needed them, but because she didn't like to wait for the commercials to do her business?

Was he aware what adult diapers cost, even when purchased in bulk at Costco?

Was he aware that Allison and Jonathan had four children, and that these four children might end up on the street because the Indian gaming industry was putting the Reno casinos out of business and Jonathan's job as an airport safety officer at Reno/Tahoe International Airport depended on a thriving casino economy?

Was he aware that Johnny Jr. had knocked his four front teeth out playing T-ball, the first such accident in the history of the West Reno T-Ball League?

Was he aware what a bridge and false teeth would cost for Johnny Jr., who had unfortunately inherited his grandmother Trudeau's oversized jaw and thus required dental work sized and priced for a grown man?

Was he aware that there was no chance in hell that Allison and Jonathan would be able to assume responsibility for another child, a child of a convicted drug dealer, a child belonging to a relative so distant that Allison, who had been married to Jonathan for seven years, was not even aware that she existed?

At that point Chiki told her that yes, he guessed he was aware of that now.

Allison told him she'd tell Jonathan that Chiki had called, and Bettina, too, when she next woke up from her daytime television–induced stupor to have another cigarette.

"Well, that's that," I said.

"Yeah."

"Now *I'm* depressed."

214

Chiki pressed his cheek against the top of Sadie's head and squeezed her gently. "There's also Jonathan's sister. Mary," he said. "I've got a telephone number for her. At least I think it's her. I forgot to verify with the daughter-in-law, and I couldn't bring myself to call back. The Mary Trudeau I found is a student at the New York University School of Medicine."

"Really? That seems so unlikely, given the rest of the family. Are you sure it's the right Mary Trudeau?"

"All the biographical data matches." He rocked gently back and forth and Sadie cooed. "You want Sadie back?" he said, clearly not wanting to let go of her soft warmth.

"No, not if you want to keep her."

"She's making me feel better. You know. After talking to Sandra's cousin's wife."

"Good. Sadie's good for that."

"She's a good baby."

I smiled. "She is. Give me Mary's number. I'll call her."

I woke Mary Trudeau up, which is a terrible thing to do to a medical student, but it's probably the only reason I found her at home. Chiki had tracked down the correct young woman; she was Sandra's cousin, Jonathan's sister. She even remembered Sandra.

"She was just a couple of years older than me," Mary said, her voice rough from sleep. "Before my aunt died they used to spend two weeks with us every summer, and Sandra and I would end up playing together, riding our bikes around the lake and stuff. Jonathan's so much older, he was never around. It was just us two. They came up for Christmas every year, until my aunt died. I don't know what happened after that; We lost touch."

Mary grew very quiet on the other end of the line when I told her about Sandra's murder, and about Noah.

"You're not married, are you Mary?" I asked.

"No," she said.

"What year in school are you in?"

"My second."

I held the telephone receiver in my hand and looked at it for a moment. This young girl was managing to put herself through medical school on her own—she wasn't getting help from the bankrupt mother smoking Luckies through her trach tube, that's for sure. She was studying twenty hours a day and looking at another two years of the same. After that there would be a residency with more round-the-clock workdays. Mary Trudeau was carving out a life for herself. Who did I think I was, calling her out of the blue and seeking to foist upon her the baby of a cousin she hadn't thought about in years?

I said, "This isn't your problem, Mary. I'm so sorry to have called you. I had no right."

"What's going to happen to Sandra's baby?"

I closed my eyes, wishing so hard she had allowed herself to forgo that question. But I guess that's not the kind of person she was. "I don't know," I said finally. "I don't know where he is, or if I'll ever find him. If I do, I suppose he'll go into foster care. He's young, only a couple of months old. He'll probably be adopted."

"And if he isn't?"

Oh, Mary, you know the answer as well as I do, don't you? "He'll stay in foster care."

She didn't speak for a few moments. Then she said. "Can you let me know? Can you let me know if you find him, and if he finds a family? Because if he doesn't . . . I guess . . . I mean . . . I don't . . ."

"I'll let you know. Don't worry, Mary. I'll let you know."

I rested the telephone receiver back in its cradle and put my head in my hands.

"Here," Chiki said. He held Sadie out to me. "I think you need her more than I do."

# Twenty

An hour or so later, Al showed up, positively glowing with success. He had made Brodsky's client a very happy man. Al had turned up something decidedly incriminating about the man who was suing the actor. He had a wife who spent much of her time looking like she'd been hit by a bus. A few words from Al, accompanied by a well-lit photograph or two, and the actor was in the clear.

Al put in a call to a friend in the domestic violence unit, who promised to send a social worker around to check up on the woman and present her with some alternatives to staying with the brute who appeared to count litigiousness as a comparatively minor fault among many.

All in all, a good couple of days' work.

Al was only too happy to make the call to the San Francisco Police Department for me. Whenever a private investigator engages in any kind of surveillance, he or she is required to notify the local police, or the county sheriff if the stakeout is outside of a major city. The cops aren't entitled to know who we're looking for or why we're after them: We don't even have to give a specific address, but we do have to give a street name. They like to know the make and license number of the cars involved in the surveillance, and what time we plan to show up. Sometimes they even ask for a description of the surveillance team. The idea is they want to know that we're there, so if they get any reports about suspicious prowlers, they'll know it's an investigator on a stakeout. Also, I suppose, if some dramatic foul-up occurs, they'll know who's been there and whose fault it is.

Al had a hard time convincing the San Francisco desk sergeant that the surveillance team consisted of a thirty-six-year-old, five-foot-tall, redheaded woman . . . and a four-month-old baby.

"Very funny," Al said. "No, the infant will *not* be driving the second vehicle. There is no second vehicle."

Al and I usually do stakeouts with two cars. We park kitty-corner to the house, one car facing the house, one car pulled forward and using the rearview mirror. That's why we like doing city surveillances. No one notices two cars in the city. In a rural area, you stick out like a pair of Birkenstocks at a Junior League luncheon, but on a city street you can fade into the mass of parked cars. We choose our cars for their "fade-ability factor," as Al calls it. As soon as Sadie was born, I bought a Honda Odyssey minivan, like every other suburban mother of a certain demographic with more than two children. (Those with two or fewer drive a Volvo station wagon.) Al drives a Suburban. When Chiki started working for us, Al picked up an old Chevy van at a sheriff's auction for him to use, claiming that it would make a good overnight surveillance vehicle. I liked to drive Al crazy by referring to the Chevy as his "love van."

This stakeout, however, I was going to be on my own, with only Sadie for company.

"He's a real wiseacre, that one," Al said when he

got off the phone. "One joke after another. Anyway, he wants you to call in with the plate number of the rental car when you get it."

"Yeah, that'll happen," I said.

"You want me to go with you?" Chiki asked.

"You can't travel," I reminded him. "You can't travel, and you can't use the computer, and one of these days some fat slob with a hairpiece and a badge is going come busting in here and arrest you for violating the terms of your supervised release."

"My probation officer is a woman," he said.

"There's a female probation officer out of Santa Ana who wears a rug," Al said.

"I'm serious," I said. "I've had to represent people in probation revocation hearings for less serious infractions than these. Chiki, get away from the computer, *now*. Go Swiffer something."

The next morning I begged my kids' teachers to let them stay in their respective after-school programs. I got off fairly lightly; in return for the pleasure of unloading Isaac for the afternoon—at a cost of ten bucks an hour, I might add—I merely had to agree to be responsible for six Thursdays' worth of classroom snacks. Organic fruit and vegetables only, no peanuts, no partially hydrogenated vegetable oils, and at least two different sources of protein. The mind reels.

Ruby's teacher decided that what I owed her was classroom laundry service. I was going to be fluffing and folding painting smocks and dress-up clothes for a month in return for an extra two hours parked outside the Arguello family manse.

The afternoon before, I'd called in an order of flowers to be delivered to Gabriel's mother, with specific instructions that the florist not leave them with the maid, but rather make sure that the mistress of the house herself received the bouquet. I wasn't bribing Mrs. Arguello; I hadn't in fact even included a card, and I'd sent a dozen Gerbera daisies, about as cheap an arrangement as you can get delivered to Pacific Heights. All I was doing was making sure that I'd find Suzette Arguello at home, and short of hiring another private investigator to do a stakeout before I went up to do *my* stakeout, sending a personal delivery was the best way to do that.

In retrospect, perhaps I was overly optimistic in

imagining that it would be easy to do a stakeout with a four-month-old. I figured she'd nurse, sleep, maybe poop a little. It never occurred to me that she'd choose that moment to cut her first tooth. Because I was a third-time mother, and had thus adopted the Boy Scout motto as my own, I had a Raffi tape, a rattle, one of those soft books and, miraculously, a bottle of baby Tylenol in my diaper bag. Still, Sadie would neither sit quietly in her car seat nor nurse. She fussed, she cried, she whined, she insisted on being bounced in my lap. It was challenging, to say the least, to keep one eye on the rearview mirror and the other on the drooling baby while at the same time trying to be unobtrusive. I failed.

"Excuse me." The woman who tapped on my window with her ivory-handled cane was very tall and very old. She was also about the width of a pencil.

"Excuse me, miss," she said again, this time walloping the glass.

I rolled the window down quickly. I'd declined the insurance on the rental car and I wasn't eager to pay out-of-pocket if the old woman shattered the glass. Neither was I especially thrilled at the prospect of picking shards out of Sadie's hair.

"Good morning," I said.

"May I be of some assistance, miss?"

"No, I'm fine."

She harrumphed for a moment and whacked her cane against the ground a few times. She was dressed for a morning's constitutional walk, in a gray tracksuit and bright white sneakers. "You've been sitting here for quite some time," she said finally.

"Yes," I said.

"One hour and seventeen minutes."

"Has it been that long?"

"It most certainly has. What, may I ask, are you doing here?"

I sighed. It happens not infrequently that a nosy neighbor inquires about our business when we're doing a surveillance. Al is particularly good at scaring them off. He generally barks something about an investigation and they hightail it, afraid of getting caught in the crossfire. I doubted anyone would mistake me for a cop with Sadie in the car, and, moreover, this woman did not look like someone who would be frightened away, even if she thought I was with the police. On the contrary, she was more likely to call the mayor and instruct him to have me move my investigation to a neighborhood with lower property values.

"I'm waiting for a friend," I said.

"In your car?" She sniffed and peered through the window, looking suspiciously around the interior. "This *is* your car, isn't it?"

Just then Sadie sneezed, giving me an idea. "Excuse me," I said, "Have you been vaccinated for the Rombolola virus?"

"What?"

"It's just that the baby got her Rombolola vaccination yesterday, and I'm supposed to keep her away from anyone with a compromised immune system. Anyone with an immune-deficiency syndrome, or anyone who hasn't had a Rombolola vaccination. Especially anyone over the age of . . . er . . . seventy or so. She's just shedding virus like crazy. And what with the chance of paralysis and rashy pustules, you can't be too careful."

Sadie sneezed again, and my nosy interloper leapt about three feet away from the car, trailing her cane behind her. She was nimble on her feet for her age, that's for sure.

"You can't loiter on this street!" she called to me as she backed quickly away from the car.

I held Sadie's hand up in a little wave and watched the woman sprint up the block, using her cane as a pivot to hurl herself around the corner. Then I glanced back in my rearview mirror, just in time to see the garage door of Gabriel's mother's house glide open. Instead of a large European car slipping out, however, the vehicle that made its exit was a bright red Bugaboo stroller. And who should be pushing this most stylish of infant perambulators? None other than Suzette Arguello herself. Accompanying her was a young blonde woman carrying a lime-green, Chinese silk diaper bag. They paused for a moment and appeared to struggle with the stroller's harness. It was their incompetence that allowed me to catch them, as it took me a moment or two to wrestle Sadie out of the car and into the Baby Bjorn, grab my purse and my own diaper bag, and race down the block.

I reached them just as they were about to disappear around the corner. I was in time to hear Suzette say, "I'm going to keep Noah with me this morning, Moira. I won't need you until lunch."

The newly liberated Moira handed Suzette the diaper bag and went off down the hill.

I said, "Hello, Suzette. I see you've found your grandson after all."

# Twenty-one

SUZETTE Arguello and I ended up in a tea shop on Union Street, sipping green tea while the babies snoozed quietly in our laps. After her face had resumed something of its normal color, and I had reassured myself that the woman wasn't about to drop dead of a heart attack over the handlebars of her $750 stroller, Suzette had agreed to accompany me for a reviving beverage. At that point, I think, she realized there was no way to keep her secret any longer, and the only thing left to do was effect some kind of damage control.

I let her take a few trembling sips before I began. My first question was very simple. "Why?"

"Why what?"

"Why did you steal your grandchild? Why didn't you just ask Sandra to let you keep him while she was in prison?"

She dabbed delicately with a napkin at her upper lip. She was remarkably good at managing with one arm, while the baby slept in the crook of the other. "You did not know my son's girlfriend very well." This was not a question; there was no doubt in her voice.

"No."

"She refused to give Noah to me. I offered to care for him from the very beginning, even though Gabriel and Sandra both knew my position on their addiction and its consequences."

"Your position?"

"I have always insisted that Gabriel would have to deal with the consequences of his addiction on his own. We are willing to help him maintain sobriety, but we are not willing to clean up the messes he makes with his drug use. But I made an exception in the case of the baby. I even approached Sandra myself."

"While she was in jail?"

Suzette nodded. I noticed that while she spoke

she rocked the baby very gently, almost impercepti-
bly, keeping him comforted and asleep. "I wrote her
a number of times. I even arranged for a visit. She
refused to put me on her visiting list, but my husband sits on the state parole commission. One of his
colleagues pulled some strings for me. I came to the
prison fully expecting to visit with her, but she
would not see me. They tried to bring her down, but
she refused. In the end, not even the threat of solitary confinement convinced her to see me."

"Did they put her in the SHU, into solitary?"

She shrugged. "I imagine they did."

Sandra chose to spend time in segregation rather
than see her boyfriend's mother? Why did she hate
Suzette Arguello so much?

Noah yawned and stirred. Suzette bent over,
pulled out a baby bottle from her elegant silk diaper
bag, and slipped it deftly between the baby's lips.
He began pulling on the bottle, immediately calmed
down.

"But why did you go through this elaborate ruse?
Why not just petition the court? Your son is a drug
addict, your daughter-in-law was in jail. She had no
other close relatives. I'm sure you would have been
awarded custody of Noah anyway. And temporary

custody would have turned into a permanent adoption within six months. According to the law, Sandra had only six months to reclaim her baby before her parental rights would have been terminated."

Suzette looked almost confused, as if what I said was so foolish she could not even comprehend it. "We could never have done that."

"Why not?"

"A court petition would have resulted in a termination hearing. Gabriel would have testified against me. The media would have gotten wind of it, and it would have been horrifying. A complete circus," She shuddered. "The very idea is ridiculous."

I put my nearly untouched cup of tea back down in its saucer. "Wait a minute. Are you telling me you cooked up an elaborate plot to *steal* your grandchild so that you wouldn't be embarrassed in the newspapers?"

"You don't understand."

"No, I obviously don't."

It took her a moment to answer. In the meantime, she spread a cloth diaper on her shoulder. It was trimmed with blue plaid and embroidered with the initials N.F.A. It took me a moment to figure out the monogram. She must have changed the baby's name from Noah Anthony Lorgeree to Noah Francisco Arguello, after his grandfather. She lifted the baby onto her shoulder and began patting his back.

Finally I said, "Help me understand. Explain it to me."

"I can't," she said. "I can't explain to someone who has not experienced what it's like to live in the public eye. An Arguello family custody trial would have been front-page news in the San Francisco *Chronicle,* and all over the country. We would have become the butt of late-night comedians. Analysts would have picked the case apart on Court TV. My brother-in-law is the lieutenant governor. He will be governor one day, and perhaps president. I could not risk embarrassing him."

"And you don't think *this* will embarrass him? You don't think that you bribing a couple of junkies, and God only knows who else at the Department of Social Services, might embarrass him?"

Noah burped suddenly and his grandmother cooed proudly. "There's a good little man," she said. She deposited him back in his stroller. "There is no need for this to become public."

"No?"

"No."

I said, grimly, "Sandra Lorgeree is dead. She was murdered in prison."

"I had nothing to do with that." She was looking into my eyes, and once again I wished I were one of those people with the magical ability to tell when someone is lying just from the steadiness of their gaze. Hers didn't twitch or shift, but still I had no idea if she was telling the truth.

"Maybe that's a matter for the police to determine," I said. "Once they have all the facts before them."

Suzette suddenly grabbed my free hand, the one that was not holding Sadie. "Please," she said. "Please, I'm begging you. I didn't hurt Sandra. I know how this looks to you. I know. But all I wanted was to save my grandchild. I didn't hurt her. I have no idea how she died. Please, believe me."

I looked down at our interlocked hands.

"Please, Ms. Applebaum," she said. "Do you know what would have happened to Noah if I hadn't stepped in? If he had gone to foster care? Gabriel identifies as Mexican American. The baby would be considered biracial. Do you know what the chances of a biracial boy being adopted are? They are terrible. Truly terrible. Noah would have been shuttled from one foster home to another. I was a member of the board of supervisors, I know just how dreadful our foster care system is, how dangerous it is for children."

"His mother wanted him. She wanted him to go to her family."

"What family? She had no family! She wanted to punish this beautiful boy because she hates me. Well, I wouldn't let her do that. I couldn't." She spun the stroller around so that the round-faced baby faced me. His head was cocked to one side, and a small smile played across his sleeping face. He was too young for the smile to be anything but gas, but it was charming, nonetheless. "Could you have allowed this precious child's mother to make a decision that would ruin his life?"

As I stared into the stroller, the baby shifted to his side and stretched, his back arching, his round behind poking out, and his tiny hands balling into fists on either side of his head. He pursed his lips, frowned, and then smiled again, his face spinning through expressions like the pictures in a slot machine. He burped and his grandmother leaned forward, delicately blotting away the tiny froth of milk that bubbled on his lips. She stroked his cheek with the back of her impeccably manicured index finger, her touch feather-light against his velvet skin.

What would I have done in her place? I would have risked any amount of shame and embarrassment to fight for this child, newspapers and political careers be damned. But what was I going to do now? That was the real question. What was I going to do, knowing what I knew, when Noah's mother was dead and none of her relatives were in any shape to care for him? The only person who wanted this baby was sitting across the table from me.

I had found Noah, and I had come no closer to finding Sandra's murderer. If anything, I felt further away from knowing what had happened in the exercise yard of Dartmore Prison than I was a few hours before.

"What will you do?" Suzette asked as I got to my feet and gathered my baby and my things.

"I have no idea."

"That's not good enough."

"You're telling me?"

# Twenty-two

SADIE and I made it home in plenty of time to pick up her brother and sister from their schools. We could even have stopped at the market and bought something to make for dinner, but I needed to get back to my husband—I needed to see him and hold him. I needed my family around me.

The four of us—Ruby, Isaac, Sadie, and I—walked through the door and were greeted by a complex and delicious smorgasbord of aromas. I hadn't realized how much the Parent Lack of Appreciation Breakfast had motivated Peter.

"What's going on here?" I said as we rushed into the kitchen. "Did you cook?" Peter used to cook all the time, before Sadie came along and made takeout an omnipresent feature of our lives.

"Not only did I cook," he said, "but I made everybody's favorite food."

"You made four-cheese lasagna?" Ruby said.

"I did."

"And you made hot dogs and sauerkraut?" Isaac shouted, jumping up and down.

"I did."

"And you made clams casino?" I said, flinging my arms around his neck and landing a kiss on his bristly cheek.

"Clams casino isn't your favorite food," Peter said. "Barbecued oysters is your favorite food!"

I took a step back, and before I could stop myself, my face fell. "No, barbecued oysters is *your* favorite food. My favorite food is clams casino."

He was wrapped in a long, food-spattered apron, and he was wearing a Kansas City Monarchs baseball cap backward on his head. He looked very sweet, and very disappointed.

"I blew it," he said.

I did my best to recover. "No you didn't. This is great. I love lasagna and hot dogs and oysters."

"But they're not your favorite. I was going for everybody's *favorite*."

"You did two out of three. That's not so bad."

He looked balefully at his children. "Yeah, but to be perfectly honest, I was kind of looking to impress *you* tonight. Lasagna and hot dogs aren't going to help me get lucky. I was thinking I had it in the bag with the barbecued oysters."

I leaned over and kissed him again on his sauce-covered cheek. "Tell you what. You change this poopy diaper, and I'll see what I can do about tonight."

After a dinner that was almost as nauseating as its parts are delicious (let's just say that these were three great things that didn't go so great together), Peter gave the kids their baths and put the two older ones to bed while I tried to deal with the mountain of sauce-encrusted pots and pans. Not for the first time, I wished I could just turn a fire hose on the kitchen after Peter had finished with it. It never ceases to amaze me how that man can lay waste to a room. He's an amazing cook, but he never uses one pan when seven can do the job.

After I was done, and after I'd nursed Sadie to sleep, I was seriously regretting my earlier promise. Peter bounced into the bedroom and shucked his pants.

"That's a nice look for you," I said. He was still wearing his food-covered apron, and his long, pale legs stuck out underneath. He actually looked kind of cute from the rear, like an actor in a porn movie designed to appeal to the gourmand who can't decide whether he wants to spend the evening dining in or out.

Peter tore off the apron along with the rest of his clothes and leapt on the bed.

"Aren't you going to get undressed?" he said.

I winced. "I'm so tired, honey. I don't honestly think I would enjoy myself."

He sighed. Then he said, "So fake it."

"What?"

"I don't mean *fake it*. I just mean, you know— pretend to enjoy yourself. Just pretend you want to be here. I honestly don't care anymore. I need you. I don't care how tired you are. You don't have to *do* anything. You can just lie there, if you want. You can be the sex lox, for all I care. I just want to make love to you tonight, for Christ's sake."

"The *sex lox*?"

I stared at him for a minute, and then, despite myself, I started to laugh. "The sex lox," I sputtered.

Peter tried to look beleaguered, but soon he was laughing, too.

Then I said, "We've never had a period like this in our marriage, have we?"

"No."

"I mean, we've definitely fought before, but now we've been bickering for months. Ever since we moved into the house. And we're barely making love. That's never happened before."

"True."

"You know, I once read that if a couple has a baby and buys a house in their first year of marriage their chances of divorce are like seventy-five percent."

"Where did you read that?"

"In *Glamour* magazine."

He sighed. "Well, we're safe. We've been married for eight years."

"I know, but still."

Peter suddenly grabbed my shoulders. "Listen," he said, lowering his forehead and pressing it against mine. "I am *never* going to divorce you. And

I'm never going to let you divorce me. Things have kind of sucked between us lately, that's true, but it doesn't matter. We'll get over it. I love you, Juliet. I don't even want to hear you say the word divorce."

That's when I started crying, like in some stupid TV movie. Pretty soon we were kissing, and one thing led to another. Half an hour later, as we were lying side by side, cheerfully sweaty and exhausted, Peter kissed me on my neck and whispered, "You're a very good faker."

"Shut up," I said, punching him on the arm.

"Give me a kiss, my darling little whitefish salad."

I punched him again, but I also gave him the kiss he asked for.

"You know what would probably make a huge difference to our relationship?" I said.

"What?"

"If we didn't have to share the bed with our children."

He leaned his head on his elbow and traced a finger on my cheek. "Are you really willing to toss Isaac out when he crawls into our bed the middle of the night?"

"Yes."

"And what about her?" He pointed to the baby lying asleep in the bassinet. "You'll put Sadie down in her crib instead of here with us?"

"She has her naps there. Or maybe I could get one of those hammock things. Babies supposedly love them."

"Maybe."

"I'll get her out of here," I said firmly. "I will."

His smile lit up his gray eyes and I realized I had not seen them that way in a very long time.

"I have one other request," he said.

"What?"

"My lawsuit. I want you to look at the papers tonight. My litigation team is great, but I just don't trust them as much as I trust you. We've got a big meeting to go over the discovery tomorrow morning, and I want to make sure I'm totally up to speed."

Peter brought me two accordion files full of documents and left me alone to sift through the papers. It took me almost until midnight, but I finally caught the mistake. It gave me an overwhelming sense of accomplishment to solve a case. Sandra's murder, the disappearance of her son, and my failure to come any closer to a resolution had weighed so heavily on my mind that I felt positively giddy at having succeeded at something.

I padded down the gloomy stone steps to Peter's dungeon. He had laid carpets down on the floors, including a moth-eaten bear rug he'd found in the attic of the house, so my feet weren't freezing on the stones, but it was hardly a pleasant working environment. Still, he loved it. He had turned the sawhorse into an impromptu storyboard and had cards pinned all over it. His toys were displayed on shelves running the length of one long wall—he collected superhero dolls from the 1970s and 1980s. His comic books were in specially designed cases arrayed against the opposite wall, and his original comic book art hung alongside his small but growing black light poster collection.

"What's that sound?" I said.

He looked up from the long trestle table he used as a desk. "The dehumidifiers. They run nonstop. It's a basement. I wouldn't want to have any dampness issues."

"The contractor said the basement's zinc-lined or something."

"You can't be too safe."

I suppose that's true when it comes to a T.H.U.N.D.E.R. Agents issue #1.

"Anyway," I said. "I think your case is going to go away."

"What?" he pushed his keyboard aside. "What did you find?"

"Well, Macramé Man's whole theory is that you stole his idea for a cannibal animated series, right?"

"Right."

"Which he theoretically pitched to the studio in November of 1993, the year before your first cannibal script made the rounds in Hollywood."

"Right."

"The guy they pitched to, that studio exec, does he have notes of the meeting?"

"No, but he vaguely remembers meeting with Macramé Man. Unfortunately. He just doesn't remember exactly when."

"Interesting. Well, in Macramé Man's notes of the meeting he has the exec's name, plus the dates he met with him."

"Right."

"He falsified his notes of the meeting to push it back in time, before you sold your script."

"How do you know?" he said.

"Like I said, the notes are dated 1993. Apparently that exec told him his series was particularly exciting because it has the sensibility of Wes Craven's *Scream*."

"Right."

"*Scream* came out in 1996. It wasn't even on the radar screen in 1993. He falsified his notes of the meeting to push it back before 1996, because your script was making the rounds in 1994."

Peter pounded his fist on the table. "God *damn* it," he shouted.

"I know, despicable."

"I am so pissed off!"

"I know."

"I *cannot* believe I didn't remember the release date of that movie."

I stared at him. My horror-movie-nerd husband was angrier with himself for forgetting the date of what he viewed as a seminal film of the genre than he was with the cretin who falsified documents in a blatant, perjurous attempt to extort money from him and the studio.

"Make sure you tell all this to your lawyers in

private," I reminded him. "They might want to save it to impeach the plaintiff during a deposition. Don't just blurt it out in front of anyone."

"I wouldn't do that."

"Okay, now let me use your computer so I can do a quick Google search on Sandra's boyfriend, Tweezer." I could get used to this working together thing. I pushed Peter over so I could squeeze in next to him on the chair.

"Tweezer?"

"Gabriel Francisco Arguello. Let's see if we can find where he went to college. I've got to try to track him down, and I was hoping I might find him with a college roommate."

Peter eyes widened and his mouth dropped open. "Arguello, as in the San Francisco Arguellos?"

"None other."

"Jesus."

I Googled Gabriel's name into the search engine. "He's some kind of party boy."

Peter leaned over my shoulder. There were dozens of hits from the gossip pages of magazines starting almost ten years prior, when Gabriel was no more than sixteen or so, detailing his presence at various events and fetes and describing the lovelies with whom he was seen. As his exploits grew more ribald, however, he appeared less frequently, and finally, about five years ago, he stopped being mentioned. I guess once he became completely strung out he dropped off most invitation lists. Doing some heroin is no big deal, but having a serious junk problem gets you scratched off the A-list.

"Try putting in 'alumni association,' in quotes," Peter said.

Gabriel never made it to college, it seemed. He was, however, an alumnus of the Town School in San Francisco, an elite and very expensive school for boys. Back when it was founded in 1939, it would probably not have granted admission to his grandfather, who would one day become the first mayor of San Francisco with a Spanish last name.

Within ten minutes I not only had a list of the boys with whom Gabriel graduated high school, but I had addresses for all six who now lived in Los Angeles. It is simply incredible what the Internet can accomplish. I alternate between celebrating its genius and cowering in fear that our clients will one day figure out that a few clicks of the mouse can get them the vast majority of what they hire us for.

Everyone can be tracked down on the Internet. Give me a name and a few hints of biographical data, and even without a Social Security number I can have a current address and a phone number, listed or not, in less time than it takes to give a baby a bath or pack a lunch box. And if I've got a Social Security number, I can do it in about as long as it takes to change a diaper.

None of us is safe. Is it any wonder that private investigators are some of the most paranoid people around? I used to think Al was a nutcase for owning a paper shredder and never throwing away a piece of junk mail that wasn't first reduced to microscopic bits. About a year after we started working together, I bought a machine that made his look like a toaster oven; I could shred my whole house if I had to. As Al always says, you never know who's watching, and you can never be too careful.

# Twenty-three

AFTER I left Peter to his work, I found myself unable to sleep, despite my exhaustion. Part of the problem was that it was only a matter of a couple of hours before Sadie awoke for her middle-of-the-night feeding. Since I knew I would soon be jolted awake, it was hard to relax enough to drift off. I lay in bed for a while, and then I pulled out the Updike book my book club had done such a dreadful job of discussing.

Rabbit Angstrom is a miserable son of a bitch, but a compelling character nonetheless. Still, it was hard for me to see what his daughter-in-law saw in him and why she would even consider having an affair with him. By the time I finished the novel, at close to two in the morning, I was feeling pretty disgusted with the whole damn vaguely incestuous family. I put the book down and stared at the baby, who slumbered on, oblivious to the fact that I was ready for her to wake up and nurse so that I could finally get to sleep myself.

Five hours later, I woke up, the bedside lamp still on, my pillows angled for reading, my neck aching from having slept propped up all night long. Sadie had just begun to cry.

"Oh, my God," I whispered. "Did you sleep through the night?"

I picked her up and winced as she latched on. In place of my breasts were two bowling balls, rock-hard and as painful as a couple of abcessed teeth. Sadie batted at the nipple of the breast she wasn't latched on to with her balled-up fist and I nearly hit the mirrored ceiling of my bedroom. "Let's not kill Mama, okay?" I said, grabbing her hand. The other breast sprayed milk while she nursed, and by the time she was done, the two of us looked like we'd taken some kind of sticky shower.

"Where's Daddy?" Ruby said. She was standing

in the doorway wearing an outfit that seemed to consist of every single piece of purple clothing she owned. She had on four shirts, two pairs of pants, a smock, and a dress.

"I have no idea. In the dungeon, I suppose. Guess what? Sadie slept through the night, and so did Isaac and you!"

She looked decidedly unimpressed.

"I'm going to find Daddy," she said.

I laid Sadie down on her play mat and pulled out my breast pump. Within ten minutes of hypnotic pumping, I had two full bottles of breast milk, and had almost fallen asleep again. It says a lot about my sleep deficit, I think, that I was nearly able to lose consciousness while strapped into a machine with sufficient suction force to power a small Third World country. When Ruby was a baby, Peter once described a breast pump to his mother, over the telephone, as "really quite painless." I offered to hook it up to a certain particularly sensitive part of his body to test out his theory. He declined the invitation.

"He's asleep at his desk, and he told me to leave him alone. He's not being nice." Ruby said.

I was rinsing out the flanges of the breast pump.

"Don't worry about it, honey. Just get yourself some breakfast. Pour some cereal and I'll cut up fruit for you."

"I don't want fruit."

"You have to have fruit."

"Okay. One grape."

"Twenty."

"Seven."

"Fifteen."

"Ten."

"Done."

While Ruby carefully counted out her ten grapes and ate her Cheerios, I roused her brother. Then I took my usual breakneck shower while Sadie lay on the bath mat, sucking her toes. Astonishingly, she was sound asleep again within moments of getting into the car for school drop-off.

"This is going to be an excellent day," I announced as I let Ruby off in front of her school.

"Do you think so?" she said in a condescending tone, skipping out of the car. Not even the realization, which I'd had three thousand times before, that I was really in for it once this kid hit puberty, could quell the energy inspired by a napping child who had slept through the night. Granted, if I had gone to bed at anything resembling a decent hour, I would have been much happier, but it was enough to know that Sadie had accomplished the unimaginable.

The first two Town School alumni I called were out—not surprising at that hour. I left messages. At the home of the third, a man answered and informed me that the person I sought, a young man named Hilton Sprague, was at work.

"Are you his roommate?" I asked.

"No, just a friend. Can I take a message, or do you want his cell number?

Sometimes, you get lucky. "Gabriel?" I said.

The voice on the other end was silent.

"Gabriel," I repeated. "Sandra hired me to find your baby. I was working for her before she was killed."

No response, and now I was worried that he'd hang up on me. "I know where Noah is," I said.

Twenty minutes later, I was sitting next to the swimming pool behind a lovely little two-bedroom, two-million-dollar house in the Santa Monica Canyon belonging to Gabriel's best friend from high school, a man, it seemed, who liked company. Or someone who traveled a lot. Someone who didn't mind his friend Gabriel camping out at his house. Gabriel was wearing an open cashmere bathrobe embroidered with the words *L'Hôtel St. Jacques.* The pocket was unraveling and there was a large coffee stain marring the fine wool. Underneath the bathrobe his T-shirt was grimy and his plaid pajama bottoms were rumpled and torn on one knee. He was bedraggled and malodorous and did not look like the scion of one of California's finest families. I could not imagine how his friend Hilton, who clearly had money and whose house might have been a stage set for a Williams Sonoma catalogue, could stand to have him around.

"I'm so sorry about Sandra," I said. "I didn't know her well, but she seemed like a pretty special person."

Gabriel nodded and snuffled thick, wet mucus into his nose and throat so loudly it startled even him. "'Scuse me," he said, wiping his nose on his sleeve. He sniffed again.

"You must miss her terribly."

He shrugged and whispered, "Yeah."

He had an ulcerated sore on his chin and he picked at it nervously until it began to bleed. He looked down at his finger as if surprised by dot of red he found there. He pressed the cuff of his robe against the wound.

"Here," I said, pulling a tissue out of my purse. "Use this."

"Thanks."

"And put some of this on it once it stops bleeding." I handed him the antibiotic ointment I kept in Sadie's diaper bag. After a few minutes of pressing the tissue against the cut he dabbed the ointment on it.

"Thanks," he said, handing me back the ointment.

"You keep it." I gave him a Band-Aid. "Put this on your chin. And stop touching it, okay? I know it's hard, but if you keep picking you're just going to make it worse."

"Okay," he whispered.

I peered at him, trying to figure out what Sandra saw in this wreck of a boy. Underneath the scabs and filth, I could tell that he was handsome, with dark wavy hair, thickly fringed eyelashes, and one of those pouting little-boy mouths that seem to demand to be kissed, at least when they aren't tainted by oozing lesions. But there was little left of the sexy little rich boy; now he looked like just so much debris left behind after a hurricane. Perhaps what I was seeing was the devastation wrought by Sandra's death. Still, even she had not saved him from his drug of choice. On the contrary, for a long time the three of them had been a team—Sandra, Gabriel, and the heroin.

"When was the last time you saw her?" I asked.

"I guess about two months before the baby was born," he said.

"Tell me what happened then."

He patted at the Band-Aid. I raised my eyebrows warningly and he put his hands down.

"Tell me what happened," I repeated.

"She was getting really freaked out. You know, where was the baby going to go, who was going to take him. At the very beginning she thought maybe I could do it." He laughed, bitterly. "That was before she knew what happened."

"What do you mean?" We were sitting at an outdoor dining table, underneath an umbrella, and the sun was just beginning to shake free of the morning fog. Gabriel squinted against the light.

"Before she knew I started using again."

"You weren't using when she was arrested?"

"We'd been in rehab for a while before it all went down. Sandra had been clean for, like, eighteen months, almost. I was going on a year. We went in-patient together, but I had a relapse. Only one, though. She didn't let me have any more after that one time. So when she got pregnant, it was okay. I mean, at first she freaked out and everything. Like *really* freaked out. She kept saying she had to have an abortion. That she couldn't have the baby. She said we could never afford to have a baby. I tried to tell her that my mom would come around, that now that we were sober she'd definitely let me have money. I mean, it's not like the old lady would let her grandkid starve, you know? But Sandra was so freaked out. She was totally out of her mind. But then one day she suddenly decided it was all co-pacetic, that we'd be all right."

"Do you think that was because of the drug deal? That she figured out a way to make money?"

He shook his head vigorously. "No. No way. You do *not* know her if you could ask that. She made no money off that. None. She introduced those dudes. That was it. All she got out of that was jail. No, I guess it was just that she came around about my mom or something. I mean, she knew my mom wasn't, like, evil. Suzette's a bitch, but, like I said, she wouldn't have let the kid starve."

"Did Sandra know your mother? Did they ever meet?"

"Yeah. After we got out of rehab, they came down, my mom and Spencer, and took us out to dinner. It was okay. I mean, it wasn't any family reunion or anything. But it was okay. Sandra took to them. Spencer was real nice to her. Even my mom was on her best behavior. We had a decent enough time. Then, a couple of months later we went up for the weekend to my family's vineyard in Napa. We did that a bunch of times that summer. But then, out of nowhere, Sandra didn't want to go anymore. She always had a reason we couldn't go. It was like she and my mom had a fight or something, but neither of them would tell me what happened."

And then, thanks to John Updike's *Rabbit*, I figured it out. I knew then who had the motive to kill Sandra Lorgeree. I had known for a while who had the opportunity; I just had not realized it. It was not Gabriel who could confirm what I knew, however. His cluelessness was profound and complete. This was the kind of thing you tell your girlfriends, never your boyfriend, and I would go back to Kate Gage to get confirmation of what I now knew. But before I did, there was something bothering me.

"Gabriel, aren't you worried about your baby? Don't you wonder where he is?"

He shifted nervously in his seat. "I know she was real worried," he mumbled.

"Aren't you?"

He sighed. "Sandra said these Christian fundamentalists got him."

"That's what she was afraid of, yes."

He shrugged. "Would that be so bad? I mean, look at me." He waved a limp hand up and down in front of his face. "Maybe if he's raised by them he won't end up like me."

I got to my feet and picked up the car seat where Sadie still slept. Gabriel stayed slumped in his chair. "He's with your mother," I said.

"What?"

"Your mother has him. Noah is in San Francisco living with your mother. Is that okay with you? Is that what you want?"

He shrugged. He said, "I don't know. I mean, there's nothing I can do about it. What do you want me to do?"

I had no idea how to answer that question.

# Twenty-four

"How did you find out?" Kate Gage said. We sat once again at a table at Swork, listening this time to the Polyphonic Spree on the stereo system. She seemed unsurprised to see me, as if she had been waiting for me to return for a while.

I opened my mouth, about to launch into an explanation of the literary inspiration for my solving of the crime, but instead I said, "How long were Sandra and her father-in-law sleeping together?"

"He wasn't really her father-in-law. She and Gabriel weren't married, and Spencer Loft is just Gabriel's stepfather, so it wasn't incest or anything. It only happened a few times, while they were visiting the family vineyard in Napa Valley. She stopped it as soon as she got pregnant."

"Did Suzette know?"

Kate shook her head, vehemently, her dangling earrings striking her cheek. "No! Of course not. She'd have killed them both if she found out. And neither did Gabriel. He would have killed *himself*. Sandra never wanted anybody to find out. All she wanted was enough money to take care of the baby. She wasn't even going to ask for that, but I convinced her that Loft owed it to her."

"When did she ask him for the money?"

"Before she was arrested. It got ugly. At first he insisted the baby wasn't his, but she threatened to have a paternity test done. Then he agreed to pay her. She was so smart about it. She wouldn't take a lump sum. She knew herself, and she knew Gabriel. She knew they couldn't withstand the temptation of having that kind of money lying around. She insisted that Loft arrange for monthly payments, and she said she wanted the agreement in writing, so that he couldn't just stop paying one day if he felt like it."

Pragmatic, self-aware, and hard-nosed Sandra. It was precisely this quality of realistic practicality that had, I knew, gotten her killed.

"What happened after she was arrested?" I asked.

"It all kind of went to hell. Sandra didn't know what was going to happen to the baby. She had no idea who was going to take him."

"She didn't want Gabriel to take him?"

"Of course not. Without Sandra, Gabriel's just a junkie. She knew that. And she was terrified Gabriel's mother would take him. She didn't like Suzette, but worse, she was worried that Suzette would find out he was Spencer's baby, and not her grandson at all."

"That's when she thought of her Aunt Bettina?"

"Yeah, Sandra thought that if she could find her aunt, maybe she'd be willing to take the baby. She figured that if Spencer gave her aunt the child-support payments it would make taking Noah more attractive."

"Did she ever get anything in writing from Spencer about the child support?"

"No, I think she was still waiting for that. She wrote him from jail, I know that. But he never wrote her back. That's when she started to panic. She even wanted me to call him for her, but I was too afraid."

Kate's fear probably saved her life.

"Like I said, when she hadn't heard from Spencer for a while, she got really desperate. I think . . . I'm pretty sure she threatened him. I think she told him that if he didn't find her aunt and pay her to take Noah, she would tell Suzette about the baby. I think she even said she'd go to the newspapers."

"You think? Why do you think so?"

She lowered her face and stared at the fingers she was knotting and unknotting in her lap. She whispered, "Because that's what I told her to do."

"I never thought he'd kill her," Kate whispered. "I mean, how could he have done it? He's a rich white guy from Pacific Heights. How could he have gotten into Dartmore Prison?"

"It was an Aryan Brotherhood hit."

"So? How would Loft know anyone in the Aryan Brotherhood?"

"Spencer Loft is a member of the Parole Commission. He must have sat on hundreds of hearings over the years involving members of the Aryan Brotherhood. It was the easiest thing in the world for him to pull a file. He didn't even need to pay them off. All he needed to do was promise a sympathetic ear at someone's parole hearing."

Kate's pale face grew pale under its jaundice. "What's going to happen now?" she said.

I was terribly afraid of the answer to that question. I knew what I was going to do. My way was clear. Al and I would call one of those FBI agents who had liked me back in the day, one I hadn't cross-examined. We would explain what we'd discovered, we'd encourage a corruption investigation based on the fact that Spencer Loft was a parole commissioner. Al would make some calls to friends on the force and encourage them to look to Loft in the murder investigation at Dartmore, as well. And perhaps there would be sufficient evidence to indict Spencer Loft. Perhaps there would even be enough to convict him. One thing was for sure, the news media would grab this in their teeth and run wild with it. The case had all the makings of yet another trial of the century—murder, drugs, sex, wealth, power. What more could the viewing public ask for?

What I didn't know was what would happen to that tiny baby in the red Bugaboo stroller. Who would take care of him now? Who would love him and feed him? Who would raise him to be the man his father never was, the man his mother had wanted him to be?

That question, I had no answer for.

# Twenty-five

I took my last trip to San Francisco a couple of weeks later. I was surprised that Suzette Arguello had agreed to see me. I made the call on a whim, more or less, because I could not get the fate of Noah Lorgeree out of my mind, unsurprising since the faces of his dead mother, his real father, and the other players in this family drama were in the newspapers nearly every day for a while. I left Sadie behind this time, worried about appearing with a baby at this lunch, and also worried that Suzette might be attended by the phalanx of reporters I feared were a feature of her life now.

We met per her instructions not at her house but

at a restaurant in a private club. There was the most discreet of signs on the door, and the elevator operator only whisked me up to the top floor of the building once my name had been checked and double-checked by the doormen and security guards manning the front desk. Suzette had arrived before me and sat at a table in a far corner of the restaurant. I would not have recognized her. She wore a dark wig and had subtly altered the shape of her face with makeup. The woman would have made a good spy.

"Hello," I said as I sat down.

"We're drinking Signorello chardonnay," she said. "It's their 1997, and it's very good."

"Thank you," I said, taking a sip. It was good, although quite frankly if it had come from a box with a spigot, I probably wouldn't have been able to taste the difference.

"Thank you for agreeing to see me," I said.

"I was curious to see what my reaction would be to the woman who ruined my life."

I paused, a mouthful of wine rolling on my tongue. I swallowed the now bitter drink. "And what is it?"

"Strange. I feel very little."

"I'm sorry."

"You're sorry?"

"I'm sorry that your husband slept with your son's girlfriend, and I am even sorrier that he murdered her. . . ."

"Allegedly."

"Allegedly. I am terribly sorry for that. I'm not sorry, though, for my role in uncovering what happened. I owed that to Sandra."

She frowned and sipped her wine. "I think this wine is even finer than I remember. Don't you think it's a fine wine?"

"Yes."

"What can I do for you, Ms. Applebaum?"

"I came to talk to you about the baby. About Noah." Her glass clacked against her teeth and she lowered it to the table. "Where is he?" I asked softly.

She blinked. "With Moira," she said finally. "In Napa."

I had said nothing to the police about the baby theft. I'd started to, once or twice, but then I'd stopped. It seemed inevitable that it would all come out with the rest of the investigation, that once they turned their eye on the case everything would come clear. But miraculously, so far I had seen no mention of Nancy and Jason McDonnell in any of the media coverage of Sandra's murder.

"What are you going to do about him?" I asked.

She shook her head. "I don't know. I suppose I've been waiting for them to take him away."

I took another sip of wine. "Do you want them to take him away?" I asked.

"I don't know."

"Ms. Arguello, I know that this baby, Noah, is about as unrelated to you as any child could be. I can see why he might symbolize for you everything terrible about what has happened to your life—your husband's betrayal, your very public humiliation. But I also know that I saw you with him. I saw you hold him and feed him. I saw you stroke his cheek and wipe his lips. I think you love Noah. Those feelings aren't dependent on a shared genetic code, are they?"

She pressed her narrow lips together and shook her head. "You don't know me, Ms. Applebaum. You don't know what kind of mother I am."

"That's true, I don't know what kind of mother you were. I know that your son Gabriel is a disaster, but I also know that our children are who they are, and there is often not much we can do to change or rescue them. Maybe you made some mistakes. We all do. Maybe your mistakes were particularly bad ones. Maybe they were what caused Gabriel to turn out the way he did. But don't you want a second chance? Don't you want the opportunity to try again? Everyone deserves a shot at redemption."

She took another sip of her wine.

"Why is this so important to you?" she asked.

I shrugged. "I can't bear to see that baby get lost. He has no one. Not a single soul in this world. I guess I'd like to see at least one person come out of this horror with something to show for it. I want someone to be redeemed."

"And which of us would be redeemed, Ms. Applebaum? Noah, or I?"

"You tell me, Ms. Arguello. You tell me."

# Twenty-six

I wish I could say that it was so easy. I wish I could say that the ending was simple and happy for Noah and for the woman who once thought of herself as his grandmother. But in real life endings are never quite as happy as we wish they would be. The elaborate ruse Suzette Arguello used to take the baby she thought was her grandchild did, of course, come to light. Nancy and Jason McDonnell turned state's evidence and agreed to testify against Suzette. Suzette in turn accepted a plea bargain that resulted in a three-month period of incarceration, avoiding the much longer kidnapping charge she could have faced.

Spencer Loft's attorneys did a remarkable job, and had things proceeded as he had imagined, the grand jury might never have returned an indictment against him. Although he might have failed in his attempt to silence the story of their affair, he might have avoided punishment for his girlfriend's murder. Spencer Loft was a hubristic man, however, and his promises exceeded his power. The man whose freedom Loft had guaranteed in return for Sandra's murder came up for parole and was denied. That meant all bets were off. The Aryan Brotherhood was eager to turn against Loft, and the district attorney happy to accept their assistance. Spencer Loft was convicted of second degree murder. I imagine that he is serving his sentence in a lonely cell in the SHU. It is far too dangerous for him to be in the general population.

And Noah? Despite the horrible irony, custody of Noah was initially given to his biological father, Loft, and revoked only after the guilty verdict. By then Suzette had come home from serving her own sentence. That is how *In re: Noah,* once Lorgeree, and then Arguello, and now Loft began. I suppose that Noah Loft is the name under which the boy will be registered at the Town School for Boys, if

Suzette wins the case. Her opponents in the litigation are Sandra Lorgeree's brother Jonathan and his wife Allison. At first I followed the case, but when the talking heads on Court TV began to speculate that the hefty child-support obligation of the incarcerated father might be the motivation for the uncle's petition for custody, I had to turn it off. The story of this little baby was too tragic. It was only by imagining him caught between two families who wanted to love him, not two families who wanted merely to take advantage of him, that I could bear it at all.

Long before the resolution of the case was clear, on the evening of the day I saw Suzette Arguello for the last time, Sadie was fast asleep in her baby hammock and my two other lucky and loved children were settled in their rooms, either sleeping or doing a good facsimile of it.

Peter and I curled up together in our own bed, and I nestled my head against his chest.

"What a horrible case this was," he said, stroking my hair.

"Yes."

"What an awful mess those people made of their lives."

"And for what?" I said into the soft nest of his chest hair. "I just don't understand it. I don't get any of it. What did Spencer and Sandra destroy their lives for? They weren't in love, clearly. So does that mean that they did it because of *sex*? It just seems so insane."

Peter kissed the top of my head, but he didn't answer. He's a man, and as he held me I wondered if by virtue of his gender he felt in some deep, unmentionable part of his soul that sex is, in fact, worth it. I wondered if he believed that the hysterical passion that lasts never more than a few hours, and usually no more than a few minutes, could justify any amount of devastation and pain. I leaned up on my elbows and peered into his sleepy eyes.

"Don't be an idiot," he said.

"What?"

"I would never have an affair."

"But you do think sex is incredibly important, don't you?"

"I think sex with *you* is incredibly important. Because I love you."

"I love you, too." I sighed. After a few moments I continued, "This case just really got to me. Such a high price to pay for something so ephemeral, so pointless. This idiotic affair devastated so many lives."

I waited a moment but Peter did not reply. I turned to look at him. He gray eyes were closed, his lashes long against his cheeks. I kissed him gently on the lips and willed myself to fall asleep.